harsh pink

harsh pink

color me burned

melody carlson

For a free catalog
of NavPress books & Bible studies call
1-800-366-7788 (USA) or 1-800-839-4769 (Canada).

www.NavPress.com

TH1NK Books is an imprint of NavPress. TH1NK is a registered trademark of NavPress. Absence of ® in connection with marks of NavPress or other parties does not indicate an absence of registration of those marks.

ISBN-10: 1-57683-952-4
ISBN-13: 978-1-57683-952-2

Cover design by studiogearbox.com
Cover photo by Masterfile
Creative Team: Nicci Hubert, Erin Healy, Arvid Wallen, Kathy Mosier, Darla Hightower, Pat Reinheimer

This is a work of fiction. The characters, incidents, and dialogues are products of the author's imagination and are not to be construed as real. Any resemblance to actual events or persons, living or dead, is entirely coincidental.

Published in association with the literary agency of Sara A. Fortenberry.

Carlson, Melody.
  Harsh pink : color me burned / Melody Carlson.
     p. cm. -- (Truecolors series)
  Summary: Reagan Mercer is just trying to fit in at her new high school when she bumps one of the most popular girls there from the cheerleading squad, but when she eventually becomes part of the in-crowd, she finds their behavior--and hers--disturbing. Includes discussion questions.
  ISBN 978-1-57683-952-2 (alk. paper)
  [1. Popularity--Fiction. 2. Cheerleading--Fiction. 3. Conduct of life--Fiction. 4. High schools--Fiction. 5. Schools--Fiction. 6. Christian life--Fiction. 7. Moving, Household--Fiction.] I. Title.
  PZ7.C216637Har 2007
  [Fic]--dc22
                              2007009513

Printed in the United States of America

2 3 4 5 6 7 8 9 10 / 10 09 08

Other Books by Melody Carlson

Moon White (NavPress)
Bright Purple (NavPress)
Faded Denim (NavPress)
Bitter Rose (NavPress)
Blade Silver (NavPress)
Fool's Gold (NavPress)
Burnt Orange (NavPress)
Pitch Black (NavPress)
Torch Red (NavPress)
Deep Green (NavPress)
Dark Blue (NavPress)
DIARY OF A TEENAGE GIRL series (Multnomah)
DEGREES series (Tyndale)
Crystal Lies (WaterBrook)
Finding Alice (WaterBrook)
Three Days (Baker)
On This Day (WaterBrook)

Dedicated to the memory of Kimber Wilson
www.8thdayfoundation.org

one

A PRETTY BLONDE GIRL SAUNTERS OVER TO WHERE I'M SEATED ON A CEMENT bench in the courtyard. It's a warm September day and I've been reading a book and basically minding my own business, waiting for the lunch break to end so I can go to class. I continue looking down at my book, pretending I haven't noticed this girl, pretending I couldn't care less that she's staring at me. I don't actually *know* this girl, although I've seen her around. And I definitely know her type. In some ways I *am* her type.

For starters, she's the kind of girl who wears the right designer and wears it well. Not in the flashy, overdone Paris Hilton sort of way, but in a way that shows she has a good sense of style and class. She keeps her makeup impeccable without looking cheap and her highlights appear totally natural. She's looking at me with an expression of superiority mixed with boredom, as if I'm not really worthy of her attention, but for some reason she has set her sights on me. She places one hand on her hip, striking a pose I'm sure is for the benefit of her friends who are packed together, whispering, about twenty feet away. Her upper lip curls ever so slightly, as if she's just gotten a whiff of something that smells bad. And then she speaks. "So *you're* the one."

I close my paperback and study her carefully, taking my time to respond, waiting just long enough to make her a little uneasy, or so I hope. "The one *what*?" I keep my tone even. No way do I want her to know she's making me uncomfortable. The first step toward losing power is to let them see you squirm. I know this because I know how to make others squirm. Sometimes it's necessary.

"The one who *somehow* made it onto the varsity cheerleading squad." Now she's actually looking down her nose at me. And that's when I notice there's a slight ball on the tip of her nose and, from my angle, it's just a bit reminiscent of Miss Piggy. Enough so that it makes me actually smile. So she's not so perfect after all.

"What's so funny?"

I just shrug as I slip my book into the oversized Burberry bag that I snagged from my mom's closet last weekend. "So, I assume you stopped by to offer me your hearty congratulations." I make sure she can hear the sarcasm in my voice, then I slowly stand. Of course, I wonder why I bothered, since she's at least six inches taller than me and I'm still looking up at her. My five-foot stature has some perks, like when it comes to gymnastics or being tossed high in an exuberant cheerleading stunt, but it gives me a definite disadvantage in power struggles like this.

"Who *are* you anyway?" she asks as if she's the reigning queen of Belmont High. And maybe she is.

"Reagan Mercer," I say lightly. "Pleased to make your acquaintance, uh, whoever *you* are."

"Everyone *knows* who *I* am." She glances toward her friends, who are slowly meandering over as if on cue. Now I notice they are some of the same girls who tried out yesterday. "I'm Kendra Farnsworth," she continues in that smug, superior tone, "the girl you *barely* beat out for varsity squad. In fact, I'm first alternate. Not that I care." She looks as if she's about to yawn. Perhaps she's boring herself as much as she's boring me. But she's not finished. "I've been cheering since middle school and I was on varsity last year and if you hadn't dropped in, like out of nowhere, well, I'd still be on varsity right now. Not that I care so much, since I think I've outgrown that whole scene."

Suddenly I remember this girl with clarity. As usual, I had tried not to watch as the other girls did their routines during tryouts. It's just my way. I figure if they do really well, I'll get discouraged and lose my competitive edge. Or if they totally flop, I'll get overly confident and not give it my best shot. For me, it's better to just not watch. But I remember this girl and exactly what went wrong. She started out fine, but then she forgot the second half of the long routine. Oh, she did it with a fair amount of grace and style and actually laughed at herself, then did a couple of really good jumps that made the crowd cheer. Still, to forget that much of the routine—well, it didn't look too promising to me. And apparently it had cost her a position on the squad. Like that's my fault.

The list was posted just this morning, and since the other names are still unfamiliar to me, I only looked at it to make sure my name was on it. Despite knowing I'd performed a flawless routine and even thrown in a couple of back handsprings that seemed to impress the crowd, you can never be sure. So when I read my name on the list, I just sort of nodded, did a silent internal cheer, then went on my way. I'm fully aware that I need to play this out carefully. Being the new girl comes with all kinds of challenges and liabilities. Obviously Kendra Farnsworth is one of them.

"Sorry about that," I say in a voice that I mean to sound genuine. "That's a tough break."

She rolls her eyes, then studies a perfectly shaped fingernail. "Tell me about it."

I look at her French manicure with those white tips that never look quite real. I'm surprised she hasn't heard that French is out, or maybe she doesn't care. "I forgot part of a routine once," I say offhandedly. "It was in a state competition." Okay, that is a total lie, but I need to get her to trust me by appearing to be transparent. The truth is, I had been really worried that I'd forget our hardest routine when we competed at state last year, but it never actually happened. I made sure it didn't. But my "confession" does the trick. It causes Kendra to smile, ever so slightly, and I think maybe the ice is breaking or maybe just thawing a little. She gives a nod over to where her friends are standing and, as if given permission, they come over and begin talking to me, introducing themselves and cautiously congratulating me for making the squad. Apparently some of them made it too.

"Where are you from anyway?" asks a petite brunette named Sally.

Now, this is one of those questions that can easily be taken wrong. Sometimes people ask me where I'm from as in, "What's your ethnic background?" Because of my Asian features I've even had people assume I can't speak English—which can be either amusing or irritating, depending on my mood. Under these circumstances, I decide to give Sally the benefit of the doubt.

"We moved here from Boston last summer," I explain. "I'd been a cheerleader at my old high school since freshman year." This I say for Kendra's benefit, although my eyes are still on Sally. "And I cheered in middle school before that." I shrug. "Between gymnastics and cheerleading, it seems like I've spent most of my life bouncing around." I sort of laugh.

"Well, you were really good yesterday," says a skinny blonde as she pokes Kendra in the arm. "I mean you totally rocked Kendra's world."

"Shut *up*, Meredith," snaps Kendra.

"Hey, it's your own dumb fault," says Meredith. "We told you to practice, but you were like all, 'No, I don't need to.'"

"Whatever." Kendra narrows her eyes and adjusts the strap of her Fendi bag. "Like I told Reagan, I've decided that cheering is juvenile anyway. This is my senior year and I've got better things to do."

"Yeah, like what?" challenges Meredith.

"Like Logan Worthington," Kendra says with a sly expression. "I wouldn't mind doing that boy this year."

Sally laughs. "He's about the only one you haven't done."

"What is this?" says Kendra with a wounded expression. "Bash Kendra Day? It isn't bad enough that I didn't make the squad, so all my friends have to turn on me too?"

Of course, this plea for mercy changes everything. And suddenly these girls are apologizing, offering condolences, and practically offering to carry her books. Not that she has any. Kendra just smiles, a glimmer of triumph in her eyes. "That's better." Then it's time to head back to class.

"Nice meeting you guys," I say as I head off toward the English department. They call out similar pleasantries, but I can tell this isn't over. I know enough about girls to know that it's never really over. And I suspect Kendra isn't ready to let this go yet. The question is, how far will she take it?

It's times like this when you need a good friend by your side. I think about my best friend, Geneva, back in Boston. Man, do I wish she were here now. Not only is Geneva gorgeous and intelligent and lots of fun, but she can easily hold her own against girls like Kendra. In fact, Geneva and I made a pretty daunting pair. I doubt I'll ever have anyone quite like her again. That makes me sad. Good friends aren't that easy to come by.

Geneva and I developed our own classification system for friends. We ranked them as class A, B, or C. Naturally, Geneva was a class A. Actually, she was an A-*plus*. I'm sure she felt the same about me. My second best friend, Bethany, was more like a class B, but she was better than nothing if Geneva was unavailable.

Class-C friends are more a matter of convenience . . . or desperation. Like if you're late to lunch and have to stand by yourself in line and don't want to look pathetic, you talk to someone you'd normally just ignore. That's a class C. Geneva and I had our own private joke. We'd say, "Isn't Jessica class C?" And naturally, Jessica, who would be listening, would assume we'd said *classy*, and she would feel special. Then when she turned away, Geneva and I would exchange a knowing sort of smile. I miss that.

Then Mom got transferred to what feels like about a million miles away from Boston, and now I have to start over. I don't even have a class-C friend anymore. Oh, I hung with one for a few weeks during the summer, when I was so bored I wanted to slit my throat. My grandma thought I should meet a girl in our neighborhood, and for Nana's sake, I tried to be nice to Geek Girl, although it concerned me that someone influential might see me with her and I'd be classified as a loser even before school started. Fortunately, it seems that didn't happen. But the sad truth is that poor Andrea Lynch was definitely a class-C friend—more like a C-minus. Although to be fair, she might've made it to a plus if I'd stuck with her.

After a couple of weeks, I'd trained her to quit laughing through her nose, curing her of this totally gross grunting noise. Then, after I introduced her to a proper skin-care regimen, her complexion actually started to clear up. And I have to admit that she actually did have this quirky sense of humor and we even had some good laughs. But a few days before school started, I dumped Geek Girl so fast that I'm sure her head is still spinning. I've been utilizing my caller ID to avoid taking her phone calls, and I even went so far as to block her e-mails. We're talking cold turkey here. I'm fully aware that was pretty heartless on my part. But when you're the new girl in town, you have to fend for yourself. And I'm smart enough to know that friends like Andrea Lynch are not an asset.

Even when I saw Geek Girl in school during those first few days less than a week ago, I pretended not to know her. I actually ignored her when she called out my name a couple of times, playing blind, deaf, and dumb. The only alternative would've been to set her straight, and that's pretty harsh. Anyway, I think she got the hint. Does that make me a mean girl? No, I reassure myself as I walk into my lit class, taking a seat in the second row. It simply means I'm a survivor.

two

"YOU NEED TO START HELPING OUT AROUND THE HOUSE, REAGAN," SAYS MOM as I turn off the blender. She's in a foul mood this morning. It's Saturday and she's just started zipping through the kitchen like a Merry Maid on amphetamines. She's scooping up newspapers, junk mail, stray coffee cups, and miscellaneous items of clothing, tossing them right and left. And I'm trying to stay out of her way. I assumed I had the kitchen to myself, since she'd been working on her laptop in the living room.

"I do help out," I say as I pour my breakfast smoothie into a tall glass and take a nice cool sip.

"The downstairs bathroom is a nightmare." Mom grabs the can of protein powder that I just used, forces the lid on it, then shoves it in the cupboard.

"I was going to put that away," I say.

Mom throws a bunch of papers into the trash compactor, then slams it shut.

"Most of that mess is Nana's," I point out as Mom slings a dirty tennis shoe toward the laundry room. "You know she leaves her stuff all over the place. Have you seen the powder room today? I suppose I get to clean that up too?" Okay, as soon as the words are out, I wish I could reel them back in. Poor Nana. It's not really her fault and I know she's doing the best she can. Even so, Mom's been losing patience with her. She keeps saying that Nana has Alzheimer's, but so far there's been no official diagnosis. I'll admit that Nana is pretty forgetful, but isn't that how people get when they age? And Nana is eighty-four. What does Mom expect from her anyway?

"Well, I think I've found a place that will take her," says Mom as she squirts detergent into the dishwasher. Sometimes the way she talks about her mother really worries me. Like Nana's an old dog or a broken piece of furniture that needs to be discarded. It's scary. I mean, I wonder what she'd do with me if I got sick.

"What do you mean *a place*?" I study my mother carefully as I envision my grandmother locked up in some horrible loony bin. Mom's hinted about something like this, but is she really serious?

"Come on, Reagan." Mom uses her I-want-you-to-play-along-with-me voice. "You know that Nana needs *special* care now. Especially since this move. It's been stressful to her and she's easily disoriented. Lately she's been losing everything. It took me an hour to find her hearing aid last week, and she forgot to put on her shoes when she went outside yesterday."

"So?" I take another sip. "Lots of people go barefoot."

"What do we do when she forgets to put on her pants?"

I laugh. "Big deal. An old lady goes to the mailbox in her underwear. I'm sure it's happened before."

"Not in *this* neighborhood." Mom stands up straight and looks out the kitchen window that overlooks the immaculately landscaped backyard. Just like every other immaculately landscaped yard in this subdivision. I've never lived in a place like this before. In Boston we lived in a high-rise condominium with a doorman and no yard. At first I thought having a yard might be cool, especially since this yard came with a nice big pool. But when I saw that the house was just a cookie-cutter version of every other one in the neighborhood, I wasn't so sure.

"My mom hates it here," Andrea confessed to me shortly after we met. "She says she feels like a Stepford wife. Like if she doesn't put the garbage can out at just the right time, facing the right direction, just the right distance from the curb, and then get it back off the street within an hour of pickup time, well, it might make her look bad." She laughed. "Like who cares what you do with your trash? I mean, would it be better to just let it pile up in your house?"

"Reagan?" My mom's voice has that tone that suggests I might've been ignoring her again. "Are you listening to me?"

"What?" I study her face, trying to remember what we were talking about just now. She looks so pale and old without her usual makeup. Despite the fact that she's had two very expensive facelifts in the past five years and uses every product imaginable to "slow down the effects of aging," her years seem to be catching up with her. And, although she refuses to acknowledge it, I know for a fact that she turns sixty next month. One reason I can so easily track her age is because I know she was close to the cutoff age for international adoption in China. Single women can't be over forty-five to adopt an infant. She was forty-four then and I am sixteen now, so I simply add the two numbers and, presto, I know her age.

Back when my mom decided to adopt a baby, China was the only country to even consider a single woman as a potential adoptive parent. Of course, this was only because the country was so desperate. Thanks to their rigid laws controlling family size, thousands of Chinese baby girls were dying in impoverished orphanages—a fact I try not to think about. Anyway, China must've figured that even an older, single mom was better than a death sentence.

Mom sighs in a tired way as she pushes a strand of blonde-tinted hair away from her forehead. "We were talking about *Nana*, Reagan."

"Oh, yeah." I take a long sip that finishes off my smoothie and then meticulously rinse the glass and place it in the dishwasher (only because Mom is watching me). Impressive.

"I want to take Nana to tour this place today, Reagan. And I want you to come along with us."

"Oh, Mom." I let out a dramatic groan. "Why do I have to go?"

"Because it will reassure Nana."

"But I'm not the one who wants to put her away, Mom."

"We're not *putting her away*, Reagan. This is assisted living."

"What does that mean, anyway?"

"It means they know how to take care of old people. They're set up for it and they know what they need."

"Maybe she just needs us."

"She's home *alone* most of the time." Mom closes the dishwasher with a bang. "And it's not helping matters that she's incontinent."

I roll my eyes. "It's not a big deal, Mom. Isn't that why she wears those granny diapers?"

"Maybe I should make *you* go to the store and buy them for her, Reagan." Mom narrows her eyes in a threatening way. "Do you know how ridiculous I feel going to Wal-Mart for *Depends*?"

"Why don't you buy them online?"

She just shakes her head. "It's too much for me to handle right now, Reagan. My new job at the bank is overwhelming. Everyone there seems to resent the fact that I replaced the last manager, Mr. Nice Guy, although he made a perfect mess of everything—a mess I'm having to clean up. And I'm not getting any younger. I just think it's time to consider the alternatives for Nana." She stands up straight and puts on her business face, including a fake-looking smile. "Besides, this place sounds very nice."

"I don't know . . ."

"Exactly." She points her finger at me. "That's why *you* need to come along too. So *you* can find out. And then you can help Nana see why it's a good idea."

And so I agree to go with them. Isn't this how every sixteen-year-old wants to spend her Saturday? Although it's not like I have a life anyway. I mean, despite making the cheerleading squad yesterday, it's not like I've made any real friends yet. Maybe after next week, I tell myself as I get dressed to tour the old-folks' home, maybe after we start to practice and stuff, then I'll get to know the other cheerleaders and things will start to look up. I know I need to make a plan. I need to pick out someone I think would be easy to befriend. I'll look for a cheerleader who, like me, is a little on the outside. I'll be extra nice and encouraging and it will be a start. And if I don't really like her—if she turns out to be a class-B friend or less—then she might just be a stepping-stone to the next friend. A class-A friend.

Naturally, thinking about this makes me miss my old best friend, Geneva. I've tried to call her a couple of times this week, but all I get is her voice mail. I decide to try her again. But, as usual, she's not answering. "Hey, Geneva," I say as cheerfully as I can for the recording. "I really miss you and wish you'd return my calls. I made varsity squad and have lots to tell you, and I want to hear how life is treating you too. So call me, okay?" Then I hang up and for some reason I don't expect her to call. I don't think she has time for a friend who lives so far away. I wonder who she's replaced me with.

I feel sorry for Nana as Mom drives us across town. She's just happily chattering away in the front seat. She always notices interesting-looking people and signs and vehicles and just whatever as she looks out the window. She sees things that most people miss.

Like the short elderly lady with curly white hair walking her little white poodle. "Look at the twins," says Nana, pointing at the pair. "Aren't they cute?"

"Yes," I agree. "They even walk alike."

"I want a little dog," says Nana in a childlike voice that's filled with longing.

"Good grief," says Mom. "What would *you* do with a dog, Mother?"

"We would dress alike," says Nana.

Mom sort of laughs, but I know exactly what she's thinking. I can guess what she really wants to say. And if we weren't on our way to a place that she hopes we will all approve of, she would probably snap at Nana. She'd say something like, "Oh, for heaven's sake, Mother, you can't even take care of yourself. How can you possibly take care of a pet too?" And then Nana would clam up or even start crying. And I would get mad and start sulking, but I wouldn't say anything because I'd know that it could only get worse. Both Nana and I are well aware that there is no point in arguing with my mother. That woman always wins. When it comes to power in this family, Mom has it all. Especially right now when I need money for a cheerleading uniform. No way will I rock Mom's boat today.

As Mom turns into a parking lot next to an institutional-looking building, I realize how much I've liked having Nana as part of our family. I think of all the times when Mom was on a business trip or working late or attending some social function, and Nana and I hung out and had a good old time at home—just the two of us. Nana never worried about having the music up too loud or making messes doing craft projects or trying weird new recipes that usually tasted horrible. But I always made sure things were cleaned up and put away before Mom got home. It just wasn't worth the fuss if I didn't. I can't even imagine what it will be like with just Mom and me sharing a house. Hopefully it won't come to that.

After touring the building, which smells like a mixture of pine-scented disinfectant, overcooked vegetables, and pee, I tell Mom that I'm going outside for some fresh air.

"Me too," says Nana, taking my hand.

Fortunately, there's a courtyard that's not too bad. It's warm and sunny out here, and September roses are blooming profusely. It looks like someone puts some time and care into this garden.

"This is pretty," I say as Nana and I stroll along a cement path that only goes in a circle since the courtyard is all neatly contained within the confines of the surrounding buildings.

Nana pauses in front of a rosebush and points at a bright pinkish-orange bloom. "That's a . . . a . . ." She pauses and scratches her head. I can tell she's searching for the right word.

"A rose?" I offer and she laughs.

"Yes, silly girl, I know it's a rose." She sighs and thinks for a full minute while I wait. "Tropicana," she finally proclaims happily.

"That's the rose's name? Tropicana?" Okay, I'm thinking of orange juice and wondering if she really knows what she's talking about.

"Yes." She smiles, proud of herself. "I remembered something."

"So what do you think of the place?" I nod toward the building, where I suspect Mom is talking to someone, perhaps even making arrangements.

"Oh, that place? It's for old people." Nana stoops over to smell a pale pink rose, taking her time as she inhales its scent, then says, "Ah."

"So, would you want to live in a place like that?"

Nana stands up and looks curiously at me. "Is *that* why we came here?"

23

I nod.

"Oh. I thought Diane came to see a friend. She said a friend . . . a friend . . ." Her voice trembles and trails off.

"Her friend *told* her about this place," I explain.

"Oh." She looks confused now.

"Mom thinks you'd be happy here."

"Happy?" Nana peers at me with faded blue eyes.

I feel a huge lump in my throat now. "She's worried about you being home alone during the day, Nana."

"Oh. Because I can't remember things?"

"Yes. She thinks you could get hurt. Like the time you left the stove on high; you could've been burned."

She nods eagerly. "Oh, yes, but I don't cook anymore, Reagan."

"I know."

"Diane wants me to live *here*?" Nana turns and looks at the long, low cement building that surrounds us and frowns.

"Would you *want* to live here?"

"No!" she says quickly, taking the strap of her old black purse higher into both hands and pulling it toward her chest as if she expects to be robbed. Of course, I know there is nothing of real value in her purse. No credit cards or money or anything besides some ruby red lipstick and an ancient silver compact. Mom took all the other things away some time ago. "No," says Nana in a firm voice. "I would not . . . not want to live here."

I don't know what to say now. I'm well aware that Mom will be furious at me if I take sides with Nana on this. Especially if she's in there right now putting together some sort of deal. I need to think fast. "Maybe you could visit here?" I suggest to Nana. But she's not buying it. She just shakes her head and gets that stubborn look that reminds me of a five-year-old. I link my arm in hers. "Well, don't worry, Nana," I say. "No one will make you do something you don't want to do."

"You won't let Diane put me in here?" she says, looking at me with frightened eyes. "You won't let her lock me up?"

"I'll do what I can, Nana." I walk over to a bench and ask her if she wants to sit and rest while I go look for Mom.

"You won't leave me here, will you?" She still looks scared.

"Of course not," I assure her. "Just sit here and enjoy the sunshine and roses and I'll be back as soon as I find Mom. Maybe we can go to Dairy Queen."

She smiles at the mention of her favorite treat. "Yes, Dairy Queen! That would be good."

So I go off in search of Mom, knowing that I'm probably on a fool's mission. How on earth am I going to convince my mother that Nana doesn't belong here? And, I remind myself, Mom hasn't given me money for my cheerleading uniform yet. Talk about being between a rock and a hard place. Still, I need to stand up for Nana. It's the least I can do when I consider all she's done and been for me. I can do this. I find Mom in the lobby, where she is waiting to speak to the head nurse.

"Nana really doesn't want to stay here," I say in my most persuasive voice. "She's getting all freaked and — "

"What did you tell her, Reagan?"

"Nothing," I say quickly. "I just asked how she liked the place."

"So she knows I'm looking at it for her?"

"She's forgetful, Mom, not stupid."

Mom frowns. "Well, I didn't expect this to be easy."

"Maybe it's too soon," I say, nodding over to where an old woman is slumped in a wheelchair, just sitting by herself and staring into space. I'm not sure if it's because she's drugged up or what, but it doesn't look right. "Nana's not like the people here," I point out. "She still functions."

"It's just a matter of time, Reagan."

"Maybe," I agree. "But maybe that time isn't here yet."

"I know this is hard," says Mom. "But you've got to see it's for the best. It's too stressful having Nana at home. I just can't deal with it anymore."

"Then I'll help more," I say. "I'll take over some of the responsibility for taking care of Nana. I'll get her breakfast in the morning. I'll make sure she's got something ready for lunch too." I think for a moment. "I'll even clean up the bathroom she uses, and"—I think I found a bargaining chip—"I'll make sure she has her granny diapers." My plan is to order them online.

"Oh, Reagan."

"Please, Mom. Can we just try it? You should see Nana. She's so upset and worried. She doesn't want to be here."

Mom sighs. "Well, it's not as if I want to get rid of her, Reagan, it's just—"

"It's just that you need help," I say with confidence. "And I'm going to do that. Trust me, Mom, I can do this."

Mom almost smiles now. "Well, okay. I guess it's worth a try. But just to be safe, I'll put her on the waiting list, because if I don't do that today, it'll be that much longer before we can get her in."

"That's cool," I say with relief. "Can I go tell Nana the good news?"

"I guess. I just hope it's not a mistake."

"It's not, Mom. Really, I can deal with this. Nana and I have always gotten along really great. And I was doing a lot more with her before school started. I realize that I probably haven't been helping that much the past couple of weeks. That'll be changing now."

Nana is hugely relieved when I tell her that she's not going to be staying here. But Mom looks edgy as we stop by Dairy Queen for ice cream. I can tell she's already having second thoughts. And this makes me mad. Can't she just give us a chance? Or maybe she does want to get rid of Nana, to be done with the inconvenience so she can get on with her life. My mother has always been a little on the selfish side.

three

By Monday I'm glad to go to school. It seems like all I did was work, work, work this past weekend. Taking care of Nana is more challenging than I realized. Her laundry had piled up. Her bedding needs to be changed daily. She needs help in the bathroom, help with her food, help taking her medicine, help finding all the things she keeps losing, like her dentures, hearing aid, and glasses, but I think I've got it all together by the time I leave for school. I also put my cell phone number on the phone's speed dial and show Nana how to get me if she has an emergency.

"You're really handling this well," Mom told me before she left for work. "Maybe it'll work out after all."

I nodded as I placed Nana's sandwich for lunch in an obvious part of the refrigerator. "Thanks." Then I reminded her that I needed money for my cheerleading uniform. "The meeting is today," I said. "I'm supposed to bring a check."

Mom quickly got into her purse and tore out a check. "Is this just for football season?" she asked as she signed it and handed it to me. "Or are we getting the full whammy all at once?"

"Just football season," I assured her.

"Well, that's a relief." Then she actually smiled. "I'm so proud of you, Reagan. I knew you'd handle the adjustment of this move just fine. And you have."

"Thanks," I told her as I slipped her blank check into my purse.

But now as I walk down the hall by myself, I wonder if I really have made the adjustment. It sure would help to have a friend by my side. Seeing Kendra and her friends hanging together doesn't make me feel any better. I don't look directly at them, although I'm hoping they'll call out, invite me over, be nice, but they don't. As I get closer, I can tell they're looking at me. I'm still not looking at them, but I can just feel it. Then Kendra makes a comment that I can't quite hear, and the girls all laugh loudly—at my expense, I'm sure. Okay, it's possible that I'm just being paranoid, but having been on the other side of this same fence, I'm pretty sure Kendra's making fun of me right now. Still, I don't show the slightest reaction. I will not give her the satisfaction. I know she has it out for me. And I know this is going to be a tough battle, but I think I'm up for it.

Because of making varsity squad, my schedule had to be rearranged. Instead of taking regular PE, we have a cheerleading class, which is seventh period. I've been looking forward to it all day, but now that I'm on my way to the locker room by myself, I'm not so sure. Still, when I notice poor Andrea Lynch coming out of the locker room with some pathetic girl who's even lamer than she is, I think I really shouldn't complain. Naturally, I slow my pace, averting my eyes to avoid any form of contact with these two losers. I actually pretend to study an AIDS awareness poster on the wall—eew. And then I continue on my way, holding my head high. Yes, life could be worse.

I coolly survey the locker room, trying to decide the best way to handle this. I don't want to slink off to a corner like I'm intimidated, but I also don't want to strip down in the center of the room like I'm an exhibitionist. I notice that some of the other cheerleaders are already here, getting dressed down and ready to practice. Feeling more self-conscious than I've felt since middle school, I find a semi-neutral spot and begin to do the same.

"You're new at Belmont, aren't you?" The girl to my left is clearly studying me as she adjusts her snug-fitting tank top around her midriff. She's about my same height and has this amazing wavy red hair that appears to be her natural color. I vaguely remember this girl from tryouts, but I never caught her name.

"Yes," I tell her cautiously. "I moved from Boston last summer."

"Hey, I have an aunt who lives in Boston." She pulls her red mane back into a bright blue bungee, creating a thick tail that goes partway down her back. "I got to visit her one summer when I was thirteen. I thought it was a pretty cool city."

"Yeah, I kinda miss it."

"It must be hard changing schools."

I nod as I tug on my sport socks. "Pretty much."

"But you made varsity," she says with enthusiasm. Then she reaches up to give me a high five. "That's pretty awesome."

I return the high five. "So, you're on varsity too?"

"Yeah. Sorry, I guess I should've introduced myself. I'm Jocelyn Matthews. This is my first year on varsity and I'm still pretty jazzed about it."

"I'm Reagan Mercer," I tell her. "I'm pretty jazzed too." I glance around the noisy locker room, which has way more than eight cheerleaders getting dressed down at the moment. "I'm assuming this isn't just varsity in here."

"Freshman, sophomore, and JV all have cheerleading the same period. We'll do some warm-ups and stuff together, then we break up into our own squads. I know 'cause I was on JV last year."

"Oh." I pull on my black Lycra shorts, smoothing out the waistband.

"I heard Kendra was pretty ticked about not making the squad." Jocelyn gets a slightly mischievous grin. "I'm just glad she's mad at you instead of me. Besides you, I'm the only one who wasn't on varsity last year—plus I'm just a sophomore. So I just naturally figured I'd be the one to take the heat." She laughs. "Then I heard that she's blaming you."

"Guess you got lucky." But as I say this, I decide that I need to befriend Jocelyn—the sooner the better. It's obvious that we're both on the outside. Okay, maybe me more than her. "Hey, since we're both newcomers," I say in a light voice that I hope doesn't sound too desperate, "maybe we should sort of stick together."

"I'm cool with that. Like they say, there's safety in numbers."

We're both dressed now. And, along with the others, we trickle out to the girls' gym, where we perch on the bleachers, listening as Coach Anderson introduces herself and the other cheerleading coach. Then she does a little welcome speech, predicting great things for the year ahead. After that she gets a little stern as she goes over the rules and hands out contracts that we're supposed to sign. It all seems pretty basic and about the same as my old school. She talks about the busy upcoming schedule and how the cheerleaders are somewhat self-governing. "I think it's good for you girls to learn how to get along, to delegate, and to make good decisions. I like to play the role of consultant, and as long as you work hard and abide by the rules, I try to stay out of your hair."

Finally she introduces the members of all the squads, including the varsity boys, Chad, Ben, and Jonathan. She also announces who the head cheerleaders will be this year. "As always, the head cheerleaders are selected according to the highest scores in tryouts combined with the most votes from the student body."

It seems that most of the girls aren't surprised by any of this, although I have no idea who the head cheerleader will be. As it turns out, Falon Atwood is the head of varsity. She's the tallest girl on our squad, with nearly black hair that's thick, long, and straight. And she has these really pretty dark eyes, sort of Latina looking, but not quite. I haven't actually met her yet, but I've seen her in my Algebra 2 class and she seems pretty nice — probably a natural leader.

But here's what has been catching my attention throughout all of this, so much so that it's hard to concentrate on anything else that's going on or being said: There is one person in the gym I didn't expect to see in this class. A certain girl I assumed would be too embarrassed to show her face around here. But for some reason, Kendra Farnsworth is just sitting there with her friends like she thinks she made varsity. I have no idea what she's doing, but I have to admit this girl has some nerve. Coach Anderson never called Kendra's name when she introduced everyone and, in fact, seems to be ignoring her. So what's up with this? Why is Kendra here?

Finally we break up into our respective squads. And Kendra walks over with her friends and stands with the varsity squad, acting like it's the most natural thing in the world for her to be here. I'm trying not to stare.

"Uh, Kendra," says Falon, "what are you doing here?"

Kendra smiles, then turns to her best friend. "Tell her, Sally."

Sally grins. "Well, we were all talking and we agreed that we should have Kendra practice with us."

"Why?" asks Falon with a slight frown.

"She's first alternate," says Sally, like that explains everything.

"Since when do alternates practice with the squad?" spouts Jocelyn. I glance at my new friend, concerned whether this girl is going to be an asset or a liability. I try to give her a look that says, "Shut up!"

Kendra glares at Jocelyn, narrowing her eyes in a way that suggests she could eat this girl for lunch. "Maybe they don't do that on *junior* varsity, Jocelyn, but it's been known to happen on varsity in past years."

"Why?" asks Falon again.

"In case someone gets cut from the squad," says Sally. "Then the alternate is all ready to step in."

"Why would anyone get cut from the squad?" Falon's tone is growing impatient now.

"You know why," says another one of Kendra's friends. For some reason it feels as if they've rehearsed this little scene. I imagine them at Kendra's house, going over their lines, practicing until they have it down. "Things happen," she continues. "For instance, someone breaks a leg or breaks the rules—"

"Yeah, remember when Cassidy Johnson got pregnant a couple years back?" says Meredith. "It was right before state, and it really messed things up for the rest of the squad."

"Yeah," I say in a joking tone, "those pregnant cheerleaders just don't have the best balance."

"And it can get really messy when they're the top of the pyramid," adds Jocelyn, which actually makes Jonathan laugh.

"And you should try tossing a pregnant cheerleader in the air," says Ben, the tallest of the bunch. He gets a few more laughs.

"How about catching them?" says Chad. "Splat!"

Falon rolls her eyes. "Okay, okay. I suppose we can put this to the vote. Let's get it over with. How many of you want our alternate to attend practices with us?"

Five female hands instantly shoot up—all of Kendra's friends. Then they turn and glare at the guys, who slowly take the hint and follow suit. Finally, feeling stupid, I slip my hand up too, but Jocelyn just frowns, like she's refusing to give in. Falon shakes her head and I can tell she thinks we're all crazy. "Okay," she says reluctantly, "looks like Kendra gets to practice with us."

Then she moves on to uniforms. She's got her laptop and immediately pulls up a website that has an outfit she's recommending. Our colors are royal blue and white, and I think the outfit is okay. Nothing great, but not that bad. Then I notice Kendra nudging Sally, and then Sally speaks up again. "Actually, we found another site, Falon. It's got some really cool stuff on it. You mind if we check it out too?"

Falon looks even more frustrated now and I can tell she just wants to move on with this. But she diplomatically puts it to a vote.

"Hey, wait a second." Jocelyn points to Kendra. "Do alternates get to vote too?"

Falon seems to consider this. "No," she says firmly. "They do not."

"Sorry." Kendra puts her hand down and acts offended.

But, once again, it feels like all this has been scripted in advance. Kendra's friends win the vote, although it does occur to me that if Jocelyn and I joined forces with Falon and got the boys to come along, we might actually have a chance against them. Not that I care so much when it comes to the uniforms. The website they've chosen is the same one we ordered uniforms from back in Boston, and I happen to think it's pretty good.

"Their prices are way higher," points out Jocelyn as we examine some of the outfits that Kendra's friends seem to have preselected.

"Yeah, but their quality is way better," says Sally in a snooty voice.

"You don't want to look cheap out there, do you?" Kendra is using that superior tone again, aiming her comments at Jocelyn. "I mean, just because some of us don't seem to care about fashion and appearance . . ." She gives Jocelyn a long, scrutinizing look, insinuating that the sophomore doesn't measure up. After that, Jocelyn just seems to clam up, which I actually think is smart on her part. Although I partially admire her for standing up to these girls, I also think she's asking for trouble, and I plan to give her a little warning speech later.

"Okay," says Falon after we've made some decisions. She's obviously irritated with how long this is taking, as well as with the bickering that's going on over whether to go with the traditional pleated skirt or the flared one. "It's time to do some actual practicing. I have a new routine that I put together last weekend, and I want to start teaching it to you today. You guys can figure out the uniform details later. Sally, you're in charge of that, okay?"

"Fine," says Sally, "but we have to get our order in by today if we want our new uniforms here for homecoming—and that's only if we pay extra for shipping."

"It wouldn't be the first time varsity wore old uniforms to homecoming," Falon points out as she claps her hands and gets us to our feet. "Come on, let's line up."

I'm relieved that we finally get to practice. My favorite part of cheering is actually doing it, but there are always those other girls who get into the politics of it. They seem to love the power struggles and fighting over every decision and making a big scene. The drama queens. And sometimes they just make me want to scream. To distract myself from all that nonsense, I give Falon my total attention. Imitating her as she goes through the moves, I quickly learn the routine and make a real effort to use my best form. No slacking from this girl. Then, just as we've finished up, Kendra comes over to speak to me.

"You're sweating, Reagan."

I sort of laugh, then shrug. "So?"

"So why are you trying so hard? You already made the squad. Do you think you have something to prove?"

"Just that she's better than you," says Jocelyn.

Kendra sticks out her chin, glaring at both of us now. Then she smiles, but it's a chilly smile. "Time will tell," she calls out nonchalantly as she rejoins her friends, saying something to them that I can't hear. But they all laugh loudly. I'm sure at us.

"Great job at practice today, Reagan!" Falon slaps me on the back. "You're going to be a fantastic addition to the squad."

"Thanks," I say as I wipe my damp brow on a sweat towel. I don't know whether Falon is aware of Kendra's attitude toward me or if she thinks that compliment is going to help. But I suspect it only makes Kendra more jealous.

As Jocelyn and I go into the locker room, I can feel Kendra's eyes boring into both of us. I'm not sure which of us she hates more, but I suspect her original plan as first alternate was to replace me. I glance over at Jocelyn, wondering where she gets the nerve to taunt Kendra like she just did. I mean, she's the youngest on the squad and obviously the least experienced. You'd think she'd know to keep her mouth shut. Still, she kept up really well at practice, and in some ways I suspect she's a superior cheerleader to Kendra and her friends. I have no doubts that Kendra is choosing between the two of us. And something about the glint in her eye when I walk past makes me think she's going after me.

Kendra sticks around as we're going over the final details with our uniforms. I don't see why an alternate should have a say in this, but I know it's not worth mentioning. I am clearly outnumbered. In fact, as the other girls make choices about the uniforms, I decide not to speak out or voice an opinion. Why rock the boat? Jocelyn has shut down as well. I'm not sure if it's a survival tactic or if she just doesn't care. But as I write out my check for my uniform, I wonder if I'll even get to wear it for long.

It's like Kendra's this vulture. And she's just waiting for one of us to make a fatal error, then she'll step in and devour us. One scathing glance from her and I feel like, *Why bother?* She desperately wants me to stumble. Or maybe she'll just trip me herself. Whatever the case, I know I need to watch my backside around this girl.

By the time we've showered and are getting dressed, my stomach is feeling seriously knotted and I'm wondering if cheerleading will ever be fun again. Is it even worth it?

"Look at the *new* girls," calls Kendra in this saccharine voice. She and her friends are dressing in the large open area of the locker room, in what I'm sure must be the prime real estate in here. "Isn't it cute how Reagan and Jocelyn have paired off like that?"

The other girls laugh and make some cloaked but crude remarks, and I hurry to pull on my jeans. I just want out of here, the sooner the better. I glance over to where Falon is having what appears to be a serious conversation with Coach Anderson and I wonder if they might be discussing concerns over this alternate thing with Kendra. Maybe Falon is trying to get some support from the coach to put a stop to it. I can only hope. Then they both start laughing and my hopes evaporate.

"This is so unfair," whispers Jocelyn as she zips her hoodie. She's dressed now and putting the strap of her bag over her shoulder.

"Huh?" I pretend I'm not on the same track, although I know what she's talking about.

"You know." She glances over to where Kendra and the rest are still getting dressed.

I sort of nod as I slip on my flip-flops and grab my bag. "Wanna get out of here and talk about it somewhere else?"

Her eyes light up. "Sure."

It turns out that Jocelyn doesn't have a car. But then, of course, she's only fifteen, so why would she? I offer her a ride in mine and as I drive the short distance toward her neighborhood, which is less than a mile from the school, we commiserate over Kendra and how she's influencing the squad and making us miserable.

"Why doesn't Falon do something?" I ask. "She's head cheer-leader."

"I think she's wishing she wasn't. I mean, she did a pretty good job and everything today, but she seems sort of checked out."

"I know. It's like she's not really friends with anyone."

"That's because she's so into Caleb Winters."

"Who's that?"

"Her boyfriend. He graduated like two years ago and they're still going out. I'll bet they get married after she graduates. It's like she thinks she's all grown-up and better than everyone."

"That's so weird."

"Tell me about it. Anyway, I don't think we can count on much from Falon. Well, besides putting together good routines and bossing us around."

"Meanwhile, Kendra, the alternate, lords it over the rest of us. It really isn't fair," I admit.

"And it's taking all the fun out of everything," she says as she points up the street. "It's the yellow one, two houses up. And I was so happy about making varsity this year. Now I almost wish I could go back to JV."

"That's probably what Kendra's wishing too." I slow down my car.

"But it's too late for that now." Jocelyn reaches for her bag.

"Is that your house?" I ask, instantly feeling stupid, since this is obviously the only yellow house on the street. But it's so frumpy and rundown, not terribly unlike this subdivision. Suddenly I feel like I've made a mistake. Or maybe she's pulling my leg. She does seem to have a sense of humor.

She turns and studies my expression. "It's not much, is it?"

"No, it's fine," I say quickly. "I just wasn't sure that—"

"It is *not* fine," she says with irritation. "It's a cheap little house in a crappy neighborhood. And you might as well know, I'm not rich like the rest of you and I can't—"

"Hey, I'm not rich," I toss back. "I'm just—"

"Compared to me *you are rich*. I mean, look. You have your own car. You wear these cool, expensive clothes—I know that's a Burberry bag. And I know your flip-flops are Juicy Couture. I have the fakes, but yours cost about forty-five dollars. So it's obvious your parents have money, Reagan. To me that's rich."

"Trust me, Jocelyn, we're *not* rich."

"Well, my mom is single, my dad doesn't pay child support, and she struggles just to pay the rent. I have a part-time job at the mall or else I wouldn't be able to afford cheerleading, and I have to study the fashion magazines so that I can shop the discount stores. I know the other girls make fun of me, and someone like Kendra would tear me apart if she found out how poor I really am. For some reason, I thought you might be different. I didn't expect you to make fun of me."

"I am *not* making fun of you," I say defensively. "And if it makes you feel any better, my mom is single too. And I don't have a dad to pay child support either."

"Really?" Jocelyn looks slightly hopeful.

"Yes. And I think it's cool that you work to pay for your own clothes and cheerleading stuff," I add. "That shows that you're probably more mature than the rest of us."

She sort of laughs. "Yeah, right. I'm just more desperate."

"I'm sure my mom would totally love it if I got a job and paid for some of my stuff." Of course, this only reminds me of my promise to help with Nana, which is sort of like a job if you think about it. Already it's nearly six o'clock, which means Nana has been by herself a lot longer than usual.

"I gotta go," I tell Jocelyn. "And don't worry. I don't care about that kind of thing." I nod toward her house. Okay, the sad truth is, this *is* a little unsettling. I mean, I may be in frantic need of a friend, but I just wish I'd found someone with a little more money. Not that I can afford to be picky. But right now, Jocelyn is barely adding up to a class-B friend.

"And you won't tell the others?"

"Why should I?"

She smiles and waves, and I drive off wondering what kind of a trap I am laying for myself here.

four

I'M RELIEVED TO SEE THAT I MADE IT HOME BEFORE MOM. SHE'S BEEN PUTTING in late hours at the bank, and her car's not in the garage yet. I hurry into the house to run damage control on Nana. But what I see when I get to the kitchen makes me want to turn around and run the other way.

"Nana?" I call out as I survey a mess of what appears to be baking ingredients and pans and all sorts of things spread all over the granite countertops. "Where are you?"

"Oh, there you are," says Nana as she emerges from the hallway. She has a messy apron over a pink sweatshirt, but her legs are bare, and from what I can see her bottom is bare as well.

"Nana!" I say in a shocked tone. "Where are your pants?"

She grins. "In the bathroom."

"Why aren't you wearing them?" I want to ask her if she's gone out of the house like this but I don't know if I can handle the answer.

She waves her hand. "Oh, I'm going to wear them. But I can't find those . . . those things."

"Those things?"

She frowns as if trying to think of something, then reaches around and slaps her bare bottom. "You know, those papery things that I—"

"Depends?"

"Depends on what, dear?"

"I mean those things, Nana—Depends, the granny diapers."

She looks embarrassed by this and I realize I don't usually call them granny diapers around her, but I'm feeling desperate. Mom could be home any moment and—

"Yes! That's it. Depends." She looks puzzled. "Where did they go, Reagan?"

I head for the downstairs bathroom, the one she and I are supposed to share, although I've been keeping most of my personal things in the powder room, which I lock during the day. I only use the full bath to shower in, and if Mom's not home, I sneak up and use hers instead. When I go into the bathroom now, it's even messier than usual. Most of the drawers are pulled open, and some of the contents are strewn about the counter and on the floor. If a person didn't know better, they might think a burglar had been through here.

"They're in the *bottom* drawer," I tell her as I pull open the extra deep drawer only to find it's empty.

"I don't see any, Reagan," she says sadly.

"Are you out?" I turn and look at her and she still looks puzzled. Then I look at the trash can and see that it's nearly full. I want to ask her if she really used all those, but it seems pointless. And I am not about to go digging in there. "Is there any other place where you keep them?" I ask her, but she just shrugs. "How about your dresser in your bedroom?" I suggest. I had helped her put clean clothes away this weekend and I thought I saw a pair or two in there. "Let's go see, okay?"

Unfortunately, her bedroom looks much like the bathroom—as if she'd been foraging, and I suppose she was. But, fortunately, there are two pairs of Depends in the top drawer of her dresser, one of the few drawers that's still closed. I hand a pair to her and then find her pink sweatpants crumpled up on the floor by the bed. "Put these on," I instruct as I shake them out. "Then come help me clean the kitchen."

She smiles. "You're a good girl, Reagan."

I nod. "Yes, I know."

I hurry to clean up the kitchen and after a while, Nana joins me. If I tell her exactly what to do, she can do it. But it seems she can't decide what to do on her own. "What were you making in here?" I ask as I put away the muffin tin.

"Angel cake," she says.

"But you're not supposed to use the oven," I point out.

"I didn't use the oven." She happily swipes flour off the counter and into the sink.

"But how were you going to bake a cake without an oven?"

She smiles and points to the microwave. "That thing."

"You're not supposed to use the microwave either."

She frowns. "Oh."

"If you want to bake a cake, you need to wait until I get home, Nana."

"Oh."

Now I can hear Mom coming in the back door and the kitchen is still pretty messy.

"What's going on?" she asks as she sets her briefcase down.

"We're making dinner," I tell her, winking at Nana, who grins like she wants to play this game.

Mom scowls at her kitchen. "It looks more like you're making a mess."

"Why don't you go in the other room and relax," I tell her. "Nana and I have everything under control."

Mom doesn't look convinced.

"Really," I say. "Dinner will be ready in about half an hour."

She just shakes her head, then walks away. Normally, I wouldn't be this accommodating to my mom. But the check I wrote today was more than even I expected. And I figure it won't hurt to keep up the appearance of being helpful and having things under control. I turn on the oven, then dig through the freezer until I find three Lean Cuisine dinners. I tell Nana to set the table, although I know I'll have to redo it. Still, it keeps her busy. Then I make a salad and manage to put together a meal that appeases my mom. We actually have a somewhat pleasant time around the table too. This isn't so bad. Maybe I can handle this after all.

"How much was the check for?" Mom asks as I'm cleaning up after dinner. I tell her the amount and she lets out a dramatic gasp. "I thought the uniform was just for football season."

"It is," I explain. "But we needed tops for both cool and warm weather. It's not like in Boston where we had only one top for cool weather. And then I had to get new name emblems in blue and white, since I can't very well use my old brown and gold ones—same thing with pompoms."

She shakes her head as she writes the amount in her checkbook. "Your cheerleading is going to put us in the poorhouse."

"Yeah, right, Mom."

"Have you ever considered getting a job, Reagan?"

I want to yell at her and tell her that taking care of Nana is like a job, but I know that won't go over too well. Especially since I was the one who insisted on keeping Nana home, insisted I could handle it, promised I would deal with it . . . which reminds me of something.

"Nana is out of Depends," I tell Mom in an even voice.

"You said you would take care of those," she says as she closes her checkbook with a snap. "Deal with it, Reagan."

"You want me to go to the store?" I ask. "You want *me* to buy them?"

She nods. "You said you'd do that, Reagan."

"But I was going to get them online."

"And did you?"

"Not yet. I thought she had a lot. Yesterday that drawer was full."

"But she's out of them now?"

"She has one more pair."

"You need to go to the store, Reagan. Tonight." She opens her purse and pulls out a twenty.

"What if someone sees me?"

She smiles an evil sort of smile. "Deal with it, Reagan."

Sometimes I think my mother hates me. I shove the twenty into my jeans pocket, then grab my bag and keys and head for ShopMart. But as soon as I park, off to the side and away from the lights, I wish I'd thought to put on some sort of disguise. I could've worn a ball cap and dark glasses—sort of like an incognito celebrity. But then, I ask myself, who is going to see me here? This is ShopMart, for Pete's sake. It's not like Kendra or her snobby cohorts shop here. In fact, if I did see one of them, we would simply be faced with a case of mutual blackmail. I'd make a confused face, like, "How did I get to this store when I was looking for the mall?" Then I'd leave and come back and get the granny diapers later—much later. Even so, I peer all around the parking lot before I go inside. And, once inside, I walk around and make sure there's no one I know here. Fat chance. Most of the people I see look like ShopMart types. Older, not that well dressed, buying things like sponge mops and giant bags of chips.

After I'm absolutely positive that no one I know is anywhere in this store and that no one—well, besides the geeky security guard—is watching me, I cautiously make my way over to the feminine hygiene area. I assume that's a good place to start. Now, the truth is, I don't even like buying things like tampons for myself, and I usually talk Mom into picking them up for me when she goes to Sam's, since they're cheaper there. But buying Depends—this is a whole new arena of embarrassment for me. As I peruse the aisle, looking for the bright green package, I promise myself to order at least a case online tonight. Maybe they'll even be cheaper that way. That should make Mom happy. I finally spot the familiar package, pick one up, and put it under my arm. Then, still scanning for familiar faces, I make my way to the cash register.

I'm fully aware that this is where it could totally fall apart on me. Kendra and Sally could suddenly burst through the front door—maybe on an emergency lip-gloss run—and they could see me just as I'm approaching the cash register. I make a quick emergency plan to simply toss the Depends aside, grab whatever item is handy, and pretend like I don't even see them. Even so, my heart is pounding and I feel my cheeks growing hot. I imagine the two red flushed spots, like someone has slapped me on both sides of my face, as I hurry toward the cash registers.

As fate would have it, everyone else has decided to check out at the same time, but I quickly evaluate the various lines and checkers. I do not want a guy to ring this purchase up. I get into the line where a middle-aged cashier is handing change to a man. There's only one woman behind him, and she has only three items to purchase. It seems my best bet. I step into line and pretend to be looking at the magazines.

Naturally, one of the woman's three items won't scan and it

doesn't have a price on it. The cashier has to call on the phone for a price, and it takes forever. Then the customer remembers she has a coupon for Tide, and it takes at least five minutes for her to dig it out of her purse. Then, after the cashier deducts the coupon, she notices it's expired. The customer tries to talk her into using it anyway, and they nearly get into a fight. Finally, like an hour later, they are done.

I feel myself sweating as I take my turn at the checkout. I glance toward the door, fearing that Kendra and Sally will emerge at any moment, but I don't see them. Then I force a smile as I slide the green package onto the counter.

"It's about time you relieved me," says the cashier to a young blond guy who is hurrying toward her register. "My break should've started more than twenty minutes ago."

"Sorry," he says as he slips in to replace her. "I was unloading some stuff back there."

I think I'm about to have a heart attack. I don't know this guy's name, but I know that he goes to Belmont. And I wish I could just disappear right now.

"These are for my Nana," I blurt out. "I mean my grandma." Oh, can this get any worse? I shove the crumpled twenty toward him and look over my shoulder, certain that Kendra and Sally will appear now.

He smiles as he scans the package, but then, instead of taking my money and slowly counting out my change, he slips the Depends into a plastic bag. I want to thank him for this small gesture of kindness, but I'm afraid my vocal cords have given out on me. I simply hold out my hand for my change, then nod and make a hasty exit. My legs are actually shaking as I walk across the parking lot to my car, and I tell myself that this is crazy, that I'm being totally ridiculous, and that I'm making a mountain out of a molehill. But I never want to go through something like that again.

As soon as I'm home, after I put Nana's Depends in the bottom drawer in the downstairs bathroom, I get Mom's Visa card and go to an online drugstore. The case price is cheaper and even if it wasn't, I think it'd be well worth it.

By the time I'm done cleaning up after Nana and finally go to my room, I am so stressed that I just really, really want to talk to someone—someone who understands. But who? I consider calling Jocelyn, but I don't even know her number. I remember Andrea Lynch, my class-C summer friend, and how she was a good listener. But really, how dumb would that be? Not to mention pathetic. Besides, she might hang up on me. That would be pretty embarrassing, to have someone like her snubbing me.

Then it occurs to me that I can call my old best friend, Geneva. I haven't had an e-mail from her in days. And it's only an hour later in Boston, and she never goes to bed before ten anyway. I just hope she has her cell phone on.

"Hey," she says in that old familiar way that tells me she checked her caller ID and knows it's me. I immediately feel comforted. "Reagan, how's it going?"

"Absolutely horribly," I confess. Then I pour out my horror story, starting with Kendra, the alternate, then my new impoverished friend, Jocelyn.

"Poor Reagan," she says sympathetically.

"That's not all," I say dramatically, thinking I'll even spill the beans about Nana and the Depends, although I've never told Geneva about any of this before.

"Hang on, will you?" she says suddenly. "I've got another call coming in."

So I wait while she takes the intruder's call. I'm sure she'll get right back to me, but, even so, I feel slightly offended to be bumped like that. After several minutes, which feel like an hour, she's back.

"Sorry, Reagan," she says, "but that's Keith Martin."

"Keith Martin?" I say in surprise. Geneva's had a crush on Keith since sophomore year. What's he doing calling her?

"We just started going out last week," she says happily. "Anyway, if you don't mind, I'd love to take his call." She sort of giggles. "Of course, I know you'll understand."

"Oh, yeah, sure," I say. "Tell Keith hey for me."

"Of course!"

And, just like that, I'm cut off. She doesn't even say good-bye or, "I'll call you back," or anything. And suddenly I feel very, very lonely. I also feel very, very sorry for myself. Usually I'm a pretty feisty girl. I'm what you might even call a fighter—well, in a peaceful way. And I usually work hard to get my way. But tonight, I feel tired and slightly beat up. Tonight, I wonder if it's really worth the struggle.

Still, I tell myself as I launch into my homework, *tomorrow is a new day.* And Jocelyn may not be a perfect class-A sort of friend, but she's a beginning. Besides, I can't let someone like Kendra Farnsworth get the best of me!

five

Somehow I manage to make it to the end of the week without falling totally apart. Even so, it isn't easy. For one thing, Nana takes a lot more time and energy than I ever imagined. And although she hasn't attempted any more cooking projects, she constantly loses things. Then she looks for them everywhere and leaves this horrible trail of messes behind. Messes that I get to clean up. I'm almost willing to admit that maybe Mom is right about her. Still, I don't like to give in so easily. And I know it will hurt Nana deeply to be forced into the nursing home. I feel like it's up to me to hold things together.

Besides the Nana dilemma, there's Jocelyn. Oh, she's okay for a friend and she's maybe even a class B-plus. She's actually sort of fun when it's just the two of us, and she appreciates me giving her rides and even takes my fashion tips and wardrobe suggestions. But when we're with others, she can be pretty high maintenance. For one thing, there's her big, fat mouth. I'm not sure if it's her redhead temperament or what, but the girl does like to voice her opinion. And that can be extremely dangerous. Now, the upside of this is that she makes a good decoy for me. It almost seems that Kendra is changing her focus from me to Jocelyn. Still, it's not easy being with Jocelyn, especially when she steps on Kendra's toes.

Like today, while we were practicing for tonight's game. As usual, Kendra the Alternate was there and, as usual, she was being Miss Know-It-All.

"That's not how we ended the fight song last year," she called out to no one in particular after we'd already gone through the routine about four times and were, in my opinion, looking pretty good.

"What?" Falon put her hands on her hips and frowned at Kendra.

Then Kendra went into this detailed explanation of how they did a mock pyramid with the bottom row of girls doing splits, the next row of girls hunched over, and one girl on top.

"Which was thoroughly unimpressive," said Jocelyn, patting her mouth as if to suppress a yawn.

Kendra walked over to face off with Jocelyn. "Says who, little Miss Junior Varsity?"

"I just happen to remember that it wasn't a very lively ending to the fight song, that's all." Jocelyn stepped back. "I think Falon's ending is way better."

I was tempted to agree with her, but then I'd never seen the old routine, plus I wasn't eager to remind Kendra I was on her hate list. But I felt like our current ending—a full pyramid with me on top doing a flip to dismount and the others doing handsprings—was pretty dynamic.

"It's the *fight* song," said Falon. "We need it to end with a real wow factor, Kendra. Last year's was so, you know, ho-hum. I came up with this ending last summer at cheerleading camp and I think it's good."

"I do too," I chimed in, hoping to sound more in support of Falon than in opposition of Kendra.

"Besides," said Jocelyn, "I don't see why an *alternate* gets to have a say in any of this. I mean, it's not like you're even on the squad, Kendra."

Okay, now I wanted to step back and just get out of the way. What was Jocelyn trying to do anyway? Start a war?

"Fine!" snapped Kendra. Then she turned on her heel and walked out. Now, part of me was thrilled, but another part was saying, "Watch out!" Because I knew we hadn't seen the last of our alternate yet.

And now as I'm giving Jocelyn a ride to tonight's away game, I warn her to watch her backside too. "Kendra looked pretty furious," I say. "No telling what that girl might say or do."

"Do you think she'll even be at the game?" asks Jocelyn as she fiddles with the hem of her blue skirt. We're wearing last year's uniforms, and other than being a little worn, they're really not all that bad. However, if I'd been around to see them for a whole season, I might think differently.

"I don't know why not." I check out my reflection in the rearview mirror as I wait for the traffic light to change. My hair is still sleekly pulled back in a perfect ponytail. But suddenly I'm wondering if that looks too severe. I'm temped to pull the whole thing out except that I probably have a kink in my hair by now.

"I'll tell you why not," says Jocelyn. "Because she's not in uniform. Her pride won't be able to bear sitting up in the stands and watching us."

I scrutinize the color of my lip gloss now. It looked perfect in the mirror at home, but I'm not so sure anymore. "Maybe she'll sneak out last year's uniform and wear it."

"Yeah, that'd be pretty funny." Jocelyn laughs. "Hey, the light's green, gorgeous. Quit admiring yourself and let's go."

I step on the gas, which makes the tires squeal, and then I feel even sillier. "I wasn't *admiring* myself."

"Yeah, right."

"I really wasn't," I insist. "The truth is, I am having an inferiority meltdown. I'm wishing I'd left my hair down and obsessing over my lip gloss."

This really makes Jocelyn laugh. "Well, don't worry, Reagan. You look totally beautiful. And you know me, I don't hand out compliments very easily."

"Thanks." I turn and glance at her. "You look great too."

"What about that zit on my chin?" She pulls down the visor and examines herself. "Is it showing up?"

"No," I say, which is a lie. Despite her attempt to cover it up, I noticed it right away. "But if it starts to show up before the game is over, I have a really great cover stick. You can't even sweat it off."

"Cool. Can I use some now?"

I gladly hand her my bag. Call me shallow, but because she's my only friend at the moment, and even if she isn't a class A, I'd like her to look as good as possible. "It's in the zipper pocket."

By the time we get to the parking lot, Jocelyn's zit is barely noticeable. But I'm still a bundle of nerves. I tell myself that this is nothing new. I've been cheering for years, I've been practicing at home, I know all of the routines by heart, I can do this.

"Nervous?" asks Jocelyn as I lock my car.

"No," I lie. Why give in to it? Oh, I suppose if I were with someone like Geneva, I could be more honest, but this is only Jocelyn.

I can hear the pep band warming up as we walk toward the stadium. It's been a fairly warm day, but there's a slight nip in the air and I can smell smoke from what I'm guessing is someone's leaf fire. It feels like autumn. Other than those few regular die-hard fans, the kind of people who want a certain seat, the stadium is still fairly empty.

"There are Sally, Meredith, and Falon," says Jocelyn, waving to the three of them down by the chain-link fence that separates the bleachers from the field.

"And there are the guys." I point over to where Chad, Ben, and Jonathan are taping up a big blue and white Go Belmont Cougars! sign.

"I don't see Kendra anywhere," says Jocelyn.

"That doesn't mean she won't come."

Soon we're down on the track with the rest of the cheerleaders, but with the exception of Falon, who is civil, they're definitely giving Jocelyn and me the chill factor. And when we start doing some casual clapping chants just to warm the crowd up, I can tell that the other girls are trying to squeeze Jocelyn and me to the ends of the line. I catch Jocelyn's eye and she seems aware of this too. The guys don't really seem to be in on it, but I can see both Sally and Meredith going out of their way to charm and even flirt with them, almost as if they're trying to win them over, as if they're drawing lines now, and Jocelyn and I are supposed to remain on the outside.

Between cheers, Jocelyn comes over and grabs my arm. "What are we supposed to do about this?"

I just shrug, smiling in case anyone is watching. "Not much we can do. Just be good sports and keep smiling and cheering. Keep your enthusiasm level up."

"Well, it stinks."

"I know," I say, still keeping that smile pasted to my face. Then Falon gives us the command and we are jumping and getting ourselves into place for another cheer. At least we have assigned positions for this choreographed routine, and because Jocelyn and I are the shortest, we're almost always in the middle. But as soon as the cheer ends and we finish our jumps, we are both jostled back to the edges of the group. Outsiders again. I wonder if Falon even notices. But then she seems so obsessed with keeping everything running smoothly, getting everyone into place, and being ready for the next chant, cheer, or yell that I seriously doubt she has any interest in the juvenile squabbles that may or may not be transpiring here tonight. And when she's not focused on cheering, she's got her eyes on her boyfriend. I have to admit that Caleb Winters is good looking, and those two really seem to be into each other. But I wish Falon would intervene for us.

Finally, I decide to just ignore Kendra's friends. I mean, really, what does it matter where I stand? At least I'm down here cheering, right? Kendra can't claim that much. Not yet, anyway. I'm relieved not to spot her in the crowd either. Even so, it feels like she's here. I sense her presence in her friends and find myself amazed, almost impressed, by the scope of her influence. What kind of a girl can control people's lives like this?

We win the game by a touchdown in the last few seconds, and the crowd is ecstatic. Our side anyway. We're yelling and screaming and hugging and even crying. Of course, the home crowd is crushed and quiet, and their side of the stands quickly thins out. Meanwhile, our side gets more enthusiastic. We do some victory cheers and everyone is in great spirits. For the first time tonight, I feel like I'm actually having fun, like maybe I even belong here.

And for a few blissful minutes, it seems as if Kendra's friends have forgotten all about whatever secret pact they've made with her. As we're packing up our pompoms and stuff, though, everything gets frosty again. I see them whispering and giving each other glances, and I can tell they're making some sort of plan. I suspect it's for an after-the-game celebration. But it seems quite obvious they don't plan to include Jocelyn or me. Not that I care so terribly much, because I feel totally exhausted now. Not so much from expending all that physical energy as from the emotional drain of being around people like this—people who seem to wish you weren't here. That's hard, and frustrating. I just don't understand why it has to be like this.

"Ready?" I ask Jocelyn, still keeping my plastic smile glued to my face. No way do I want those girls to see how much this hurts.

"Yeah, I guess." She tosses a longing glance over to where the others are huddled together so exclusively. I know she can feel it too. But I refuse to acknowledge it. I'd rather pretend that I haven't noticed, act like I don't care. No big deal.

"This totally sucks," mutters Jocelyn as we walk to my car.

"What?" I continue my act, like I don't know what's going on, like I have no feelings.

"You *know* what, Reagan!" she shouts at me. "Don't play dumb."

"Shh!" I hiss at her as I hurry across the parking lot. "You don't have to let the whole world know what's going on here."

"Like they don't know anyway. Isn't it obvious?"

"Maybe . . . but our best defense is to simply act like we don't care. If they see us getting all upset, it's like they've won. Don't you get that?"

"No!" she snaps. "Frankly, I don't get it. This is a game I've tried not to engage in. It's a game I can't stand. I mean, last year there was this girl on JV, Monica, and when she tried to pull stunts like this, I just told her to knock it off."

"And she did?" I turn and stare at Jocelyn, surprised that she would have that kind of ability to persuade someone. Maybe I've misjudged her.

"Well, last year, *I* was head cheerleader. Monica had to knock it off."

"*You* were head cheerleader?"

"Yeah. Why else do you think I made varsity?"

"Because you're good."

"Hey, thanks!" She smiles as we throw our duffle bags into the back of my car. "And sorry for being such a grump. But it just ticks me off. It's like the other cheerleaders are Kendra's robots or something, like she has this secret remote and she controls every move they make. Well, other than Falon. I don't think Kendra can control her. And Falon could be helpful, except she's so obsessed over getting everything perfect. I wish she'd just lighten up and have some fun."

"I guess being head cheerleader is a big responsibility," I say as we get inside. "Although you probably know that, since you did it last year."

"Yeah, but just because it's a big responsibility doesn't mean it can't still be fun. I always had fun." She points over to where the other cheerleaders are getting into cars, laughing and acting like they're heading off to someplace fun. "So, seriously, Reagan, what do you think they're up to tonight?"

I shrug and turn on my engine. "I haven't a clue."

"Hey, we could follow them," she suggests in a sneaky tone.

"Thanks, but no thanks." I pull behind a line of cars waiting to exit the parking lot.

"You wouldn't have to let them see us," she persists.

"No way! I am *not* going to follow them. How lame would that be? Honestly, Jocelyn, would you seriously walk into some place where we're not invited, where we're not even wanted? Isn't that a little pathetic?"

She slumps in the seat. "Yeah, I guess."

I sigh. "Good."

"But we could just follow them to see where they're going, Reagan. We wouldn't have to go inside. Honestly, aren't you just a little bit curious?"

I consider this. "Yeah, maybe a little."

"Pull over onto this side street," she commands, pointing to the right. And like an idiot, I do it.

"Now, do a U-turn and just wait until we see their cars." So I do that, then we sit there and wait until several familiar cars exit the parking lot. Fortunately, no one notices my red Toyota as they honk their horns, yell out windows, and whiz past the side street like they think they're in a parade. Then I pull out and follow about a block behind them. They're heading back to our side of town, and when we're nearly there, they turn down a tree-lined country lane and then make another right-hand turn. Like an idiot, I turn too. That's when I realize I've turned onto a private road that goes into a gated community. Now I am stuck in a line of cars waiting to get through the security gates.

"Aha," says Jocelyn. "So this is what's going on."

"What?"

"Aspen Reserve." She reads the fancy brass letters on the large sign.

"Yes," I tell her. "I am perfectly capable of reading too. But we can't go in there . . . not without a password." I let out a groan as one car passes through the gates. Why did I listen to Jocelyn? Now somehow I'll have to turn around up at the gate. With everyone watching I will get to make a complete spectacle of myself. Just great.

"Aspen Reserve is the most expensive development in town," she tells me. "And the only person I know who lives here is Kendra Farnsworth. Her dad developed this whole place and owns at least half of it. Kendra gets to use the clubhouse whenever she likes for parties or whatever. And it's awesome. There's this huge swimming pool and game room and even a bar, which she'll probably have stocked."

"How do you know all this?" I pull up another car length, wondering whether I'll even be able to turn around in the turnout up ahead. This is so humiliating.

"Because Kendra *always* hosts the annual cheerleaders' barbecue in the spring. She invites all the cheerleaders and their dates, kind of as a way to end the year, ya know." Jocelyn sighs. "It was so fun last year. She also had the annual fall barbecue here last year, but that one is only for varsity. Or maybe she had that one at her house, since it wasn't as huge. I wouldn't know since I couldn't go to that one, but I heard it was spectacular."

I put my car into reverse, hoping I can back up a little and maybe actually turn around, but the car directly behind me is not budging, plus they're honking like they think I'm going to run into them. And maybe I should. I keep on going, backing up a few inches, as in, hint hint. But then they just honk again, louder and longer. So I stick my head out the window. "Excuse me," I call out to the black pickup. "I need to back up, please!"

To my surprise, fellow cheerleader Jonathan sticks his head out and yells, "Why?" Now, of the three cheerleader guys, Jonathan has been the nicest to me and I get the impression he's a pretty thoughtful guy. But what am I supposed to tell him? I glance at Jocelyn like I think she can help me out here. And to my surprise she jumps out of the car and runs around and starts talking to Jonathan. I watch her from my side mirror as she stands on tiptoe and leans into his window. I can hear her telling him how we weren't actually invited and then saying something like we sort of misunderstood and came anyway, and who knows what else she's saying, although it sounds lame to me and I just wish she'd come back so I could leave. I think I might have enough room to turn around now.

"That's total bull," Jonathan yells loudly. He sticks his hand out the window and points at the gates. "Of course you guys are invited! It's a victory party and all the cheerleaders are invited. Go ahead, go on in!"

"But I don't know the code," I call back.

Then he says something to Jocelyn and she comes bounding back and hops in the car. "Let's go, Reagan!"

Now the cars ahead of me have already moved through the gates, and I realize I have a decision to make. I could get away now if I wanted to. "But we're not invited, Jocelyn."

"Yes, we are!" she shouts. "Jonathan invited us!"

I consider this as the cars behind start honking again. "Okay," I tell her, pulling forward. "We're going in!"

"Oh, this is going to be fun," she says as she literally rubs her hands together. "I can't wait to see Kendra's face."

"What if she throws us out?"

"She wouldn't dare. Not if we go in with Jonathan, one on each arm. She'd look like a total jerk if she turned us away, and everyone would see it. She's got to let us in, Reagan."

Okay, I have to admit that I admire this girl's spunk. She may be a year younger, but she's got some smarts. In some ways she reminds me of Geneva. I might even move her up from class B to class A. Okay, A-minus. But it's a start.

six

JOCELYN DIRECTS ME TO THE CLUBHOUSE, WHICH IS PRETTY EASY TO FIND SINCE it's all lit up and we can hear music blasting from it even though my car windows are up. We park and wait for Jonathan's pickup, which I discover has all three cheerleader guys in it. I'm pleasantly surprised to learn they're feeling indignant that Jocelyn and I weren't invited to the celebration. So instead of crashing the party with only Jonathan, we are escorted in by all three and consequently make a pretty grand entrance, if I do say so myself.

I spot Kendra as soon as we're in the door. It's easy, since her hot pink sweater stands out amid the sea of royal blue and white. But I can tell by the glint in her eyes that she is not pleased. Not at all. Even so, you'd never know this by the expression on the rest of her face. Like me, she's good at forcing a smile, putting up a good front. Still, it's a little unsettling when she moves through the crowd straight to us. I actually wonder if she might really be about to throw us out. Oh, I'm sure she'd do it gracefully and with poise. She wouldn't want to look bad in front of everyone. It occurs to me that she probably has the right to throw us out. I mean, we really weren't invited. Suddenly I want to leave. What was I thinking?

"I'm *so* glad you guys made it," she says with false warmth as she joins us. "Reagan and Jocelyn." Her words sound gracious and she smiles, exposing perfectly aligned and whitened teeth. "I heard you two had turned up your noses, that you planned to snub my little soiree."

I am speechless and Jocelyn barely opens her mouth before Jonathan jumps in. "Don't you mean you heard that *no one* invited them?" he says.

"Of course they were invited," she says lightly, slipping an arm around Jonathan and giving him a squeeze. "This is a victory celebration! *All* the cheerleaders were invited."

"Then what made you think they didn't want to come?" persists Ben.

Kendra laughs, then puts a carefully manicured finger over her perfectly glossed lips. "Maybe it's because they heard there would be more than just soda and punch served tonight." She looks directly at me now. "Isn't that true, Reagan? You and Jocelyn are opposed to drinking, right?"

Okay, this is actually true about me, although I haven't told a soul this. Not even Jocelyn. I turn to look at my new friend, curious as to whether this is news to her. I also remember the cheerleading contract we all signed (well, everyone except Kendra). But Jocelyn just looks Kendra in the eyes, then grins. "Hey, I have no idea where you heard that, Kendra, but it's a big, fat lie. So, anyway, where's the beer?"

Everyone laughs and Kendra's blue eyes widen as if she's surprised, but she points Jocelyn over to the bar, where several cheerleaders are already drinking from cups topped with foam. "The keg's right there, sweetie. Help yourself." Then she turns to me. "How about you, Reagan, do you want to drink?"

Now, peer pressure isn't new to me. What teen hasn't felt it? But back in my own school, my friends pretty much accepted me for who I am. They knew I wasn't into alcohol, and although they teased me occasionally, that's where it ended. They never pressured me to drink, never pulled a stunt like this. Once again I'm reminded that this is a whole new game—a game I almost feel too tired to play. Will it ever get easier? Is it even worth it?

It occurs to me that I could walk right out of here. I could snub Kendra and maintain my pride at the same time. But then I'd be right back where I started. Maybe this game will end sooner if I simply play along. Even so, I look around the room, checking to see if Falon is here tonight, because I have a feeling she'd report us for breaking the rules of the contract. Then I realize she's probably with her boyfriend. I'm sure they'd think this was too juvenile. I also consider the possibility of the cops showing up, but that seems unlikely in this gated community.

"Reagan?" persists Kendra. "You want a drink?"

"What do you have besides beer?" I ask tentatively. Okay, I feel slightly defeated just now, but not ready to give up.

She starts reeling off a great long list, and I'm sure I look pretty baffled, which must be amusing since she just throws back her head and laughs. "Come on, Reagan." She hooks her arm into mine like we're old buddies. "Let me fix you a *good* drink."

Okay, this is dangerous. I'm thinking you should never, ever let your enemy fix you a drink. I'm sure this is one of the most ancient survival rules of civilization. Then again, I remind myself, I don't have to actually drink it. Plus, if I watch her closely while she makes my drink, I can be relatively sure that she doesn't do anything weird to it.

"Okay," I say with some reluctance as she navigates us through the crowd and over to the bar.

She leans her elbows opposite me onto the granite top and looks at me. "Hmmm." Her eyes narrow slightly, as if she's studying me. "I think you must be a Cosmo girl."

"What does that mean?" I ask, still suspicious.

She reaches for a clear plastic cup and tosses some ice in. "It means I think you'd like a Cosmo."

Then I vaguely remember hearing that it's a drink. "What's in it?" I ask, further revealing my ignorance but hoping it might help to disarm her.

"You've *never* had a Cosmo?"

"Not that I recall."

She's got a bottle of something clear opened now, but I can't read the label. "Well, you start with a shot of vodka"—she pours a little into the cup—"then some triple sec." She opens a bottle and pours something else in, but not too much. "Then you add some lime juice, and finally some cranberry juice, which is what makes it look so pink and pretty." She finally holds up the pink drink and smiles. "Voilà!" And I must admit that it does look pretty. Even she looks pretty holding it in front of her pink sweater, which I'm certain is cashmere and expensive. She hands me the drink and I thank her.

"It looks good," I say, unsure of what to do next.

"So good that I think I'll join you," she says. So I wait while she makes another drink, exactly the way she made mine, which I find somewhat reassuring. Then she holds up what looks like an identical drink and says, "Here's to new friendships."

I try not to look too shocked by her unexpected toast, but I meekly echo it. "To new friendships." Then we both take a sip. And, okay, it's not that great, but it's not terrible either, and as far as I can tell it's not poisoned. I figure at least I can walk around now, carrying my drink, pretending to enjoy it, and when no one is looking, I can simply dump it.

"So, Reagan, did you enjoy cheering tonight?" She takes a casual sip. "Was it fun?"

I nod, unsure of where she's going with this line of questioning. "Yeah, it was a good game."

She sort of frowns now. "I feel bad that I missed it."

"Why didn't you come?"

She waves an arm. "I was getting this all set up. I wanted to wait until my parents left before I got everything ready. Then it was too late and I decided to just skip it."

"So your parents don't know about this party?" I glance around the crowded, noisy room and wonder how Kendra could possibly keep a gathering of this size a secret.

"Oh, sure, they know I'm having a party. They just don't know about the booze. My parents are pretty laid back, but they wouldn't approve of this. Fortunately, they had a wedding to go to, and I figured it'd be easier to set things up once they were safely on their way."

I know it's none of my business, but I still feel worried. "When will they be back?"

She smiles. "Oh, the wedding was up in Wyndham. They won't get home until tomorrow evening, and I already have some cleaning people lined up for the morning. By the time they get back, everything will be nice and neat. No problem."

"Impressive," I say, and in a way it is. Kendra is the kind of girl who just seems to know what she wants and how to get it. Of course, that didn't exactly work for her in regard to cheerleading this year. In a way, I think that's a shame. To my surprise (or is it these two sips of alcohol?) I feel sort of bad for having made varsity squad, like maybe I really am the reason Kendra's out in the cold now. "You know, Kendra," I begin. "I really am sorry that you're not on varsity this year. I have a feeling it's just not the same without you."

She blinks. "Really?" She leans forward and peers into my eyes. "Do you really mean that, Reagan?"

Okay, now I feel scared. Like is she misinterpreting my intent? Does she think I'm willing to relinquish my position for her? Even so, I nod, hoping I can make myself a bit more clear. "Yes, I think I would've enjoyed being with you on the squad. Not like at practice where everyone gets a little edgy and cranky, but at the games. I think you would've been a lot of fun."

She nods and I think her eyes are actually getting misty—or maybe she's had more than just this one drink. "I *was* fun, Reagan. I really was." She makes a goofy grin, then gently socks me in the arm. "And you and me, Reagan, I think we could've had fun together. I think we would've gotten along just fine. We could've been real friends."

"Really?" Is she pulling something over on me? Is there something in my Cosmo? I glance at my drink, but most of it is still safely in the cup. And if anyone is acting slightly intoxicated just now, she is. I study her closely and for some unexplainable reason, I think she's being sincere. "Do you really think we could've been friends?"

She nods again. "Yes. I most certainly do." Then she shrugs. "Hey, who knows? Maybe we still can."

So I give her my most genuine smile. Well, under the circumstances anyway. "That'd be cool," I say, knowing I'm putting myself at serious risk. I know as well as anyone that social situations like this are sort of like a poker game. You don't want to show anyone your hand, and sometimes you have to bluff. Then there are those times when you tell the truth but your opponent thinks you're bluffing anyway. And sometimes you get pulled in and you fall for their bluff. It's all very, very tricky.

But by the end of the evening, after I've danced and laughed and met some new people, after I've had a good time and some fun conversations—some of them with Kendra—for the first time since moving here, I feel like I might actually fit in. And I think Kendra's offer of friendship might be sincere. And, as mind-boggling as it seems, I decide that I really do want to be her friend.

"Sally and Meredith and I are going to the mall tomorrow," she tells me as I'm about to leave. "You want to come with us?"

I consider Jocelyn and feel uncomfortable. Not that I have to include her in everything, but it did seem like we were becoming good friends. I glance over to where she's dancing with Chad. The place has been steadily clearing out the last few minutes, but there are still some couples on the dance floor. Jocelyn seems like she's really into Chad, which is a surprise to me because she hadn't mentioned this before. But it might just be the effect of the alcohol. I'm pretty sure she's overdone it tonight.

"Just you," says Kendra, as if reading my mind. "I don't want to be mean, but my car's not that big, you know. Four is pretty tight." Then she laughs as she points toward Jocelyn. "Besides, that girl is going to be nursing a nasty hangover tomorrow. Mark my word."

I laugh too. "You're probably right. Sure, I'd love to go to the mall."

"I'll call you."

"Thanks for the party," I tell her. "And everything."

She smiles and it really does seem sincere. Then I go and get Jocelyn, peeling her off Chad and directing her out the door and across the parking lot. She's definitely weaving as we walk, and we're almost to my car when she starts moaning and groaning.

She hunches over and holds onto her stomach.

"What's wrong?" I ask, bending down to see her face.

That's when she starts hurling. I jump back just in time to miss the explosion.

"Eew!" I yell, moving even farther away from her. "Gross, Jocelyn!" But then, hearing her quiet sobs, I feel bad. I go back over and help to balance her as she continues to barf her guts out. I try to hold back her hair and keep her from falling as she hurls and hurls. I tell her it'll be okay and that I'll get her home soon, and finally she seems to be finished. Careful to miss the puddle, I help her get into my car, hoping that she isn't going to hurl again, although it seems like her stomach should be totally empty by now. I find a couple of unused McDonald's napkins as well as a half-full water bottle in the backseat. I give these to her. "Wipe off your mouth," I tell her. "And have a few sips of water."

She doesn't say a word as I drive her home. This is a relief, because all I can think about right now is that I somehow seem to have crossed the invisible line. It feels like Kendra has accepted me, like she has allowed me into her inner circle. Oh, I realize it could be a trick. But something tells me it's not. Anyway, it's a risk I'm willing to take. Thankfully, Jocelyn seems a lot better by the time I get her home.

"Do you want me to help you into the house?" I offer.

"No," she says in a raspy voice. "I'm okay."

"Take care," I say as she gets out. "And drink some juice or something before you go to bed. I've heard that too much alcohol can really dehydrate a person. Maybe have some Gatorade or something, okay?"

She gives me a weak smile. "Thanks, Reagan. You're a real friend."

I nod and wave, thinking, *No, I'm not a real friend. I'm more like a real phony.* Then I drive away and try not to think about it.

***

Although I'm Chinese by birth, I am truly 100 percent American. It's all I've ever known and all I can relate to. Even so, I think I may have some Chinese—rather, Buddhist—traits. Not in a religious sort of way, since I think of myself as generally nonreligious, but more in a philosophical sort of way. My only explanation for this is DNA—meaning I think my Chinese DNA is compatible with Buddhism. All this to say that since I was a little girl, my way to make up for my mistakes has always been to work very hard. It's part of Buddhism to believe you can replace bad with good. For instance, when I was about seven I broke an antique rocking chair by doing a gymnastic trick. I swept the kitchen, vacuumed the carpet, washed dishes, folded laundry, all sorts of domestic things. Whatever it takes to balance the scales. For the most part this has worked for me. But sometimes it makes me really, really tired.

Like today. Even though I went to bed quite late last night and this is Saturday, I got up early this morning to do chores. I know this is partly because I feel guilty for going to a drinking party, something Mom would not approve of, but also because I feel guilty that I'll be leaving Jocelyn out in the cold by going to the mall with Kendra today. Of course, Jocelyn is clueless, and I'm sure she's still sleeping off her night of boozing. I warned her to take it easy last night. I told her she'd had too much. But, no, she wanted to "par*tay*!" And look where that got her.

Anyway, as I fix Nana some breakfast, clean up her messes, do a few loads of laundry, change Nana's sheets, and fix her a lunch for later, I somehow convince myself that all this work makes things right. By the time Kendra pulls into my driveway around noon, I'm convinced my slate is clean.

"Have fun," calls Nana as I sprint for the door. I hurry because I don't want to take any chances of Kendra or the others getting close enough to my house to gaze inside and see anything. Not that it looks bad. It doesn't. But Nana is so unpredictable. She could say or do anything. It's just not worth the risk.

Kendra has the top down on her pale blue BMW convertible. She and Sally are in the front seat and Meredith is tucked into the back.

"Hop in," says Kendra, and I assume she means literally since no one is opening a door. So I start to climb over.

"Hang on," says Sally in a somewhat snooty tone. "I was about to open the door, Reagan!"

"Oh." I attempt a small laugh at my own expense and wait as she slowly opens the front door, then pops the front seat forward just enough so that I can barely squeeze in. Kendra wasn't kidding about the size of her car. Five girls would be like sardines in here.

"Good thing none of my friends are fat," says Kendra as she backs out. "Hang on, girls!" Then she squeals her tires down the street and I hope Nana's not watching from the front window, because I know she'd worry that I'll be killed.

I wish I could relax and enjoy this. I mean, it's a beautiful fall day, and riding in a convertible with friends could be such fun. But I know these girls aren't really my friends. At least not yet. I hope to win them over, to make them my friends. Being on their side would make my life so much easier. But I know I have to be on my guard. I have to watch every step, every word. And I especially have to watch for any tricks aimed at me. I'm fully aware that today could be a total setup. Kendra could just be pretending to like me so that the three of them can undermine me in some totally humiliating way. It's ironic, because I'm sure someone could see the four of us driving by and assume that we're all having such a good time, that we're close friends, girls on the town, just hanging and enjoying each other. And, okay, that may be true for them. But it's the farthest thing from the truth for me. Still, maybe someday. If I pass their test.

"Jocelyn made such a fool of herself last night," says Kendra as we walk across the parking lot.

"Yeah, I heard she puked all over your car," says Sally.

"Fortunately, she hurled *before* she got in," I explain.

"Even so, how can you stand hanging with a loser like that?" asks Kendra.

"Yeah," says Sally. "She probably smelled like barf when you drove her home. Did you have to disinfect your car and everything?"

I force a laugh. "Well, I couldn't just leave her on the street. Then poor Kendra would've been stuck with her. And she'd have some explaining to do to her cleanup crew in the morning."

"Not to mention the security guard," adds Kendra.

"So I figured I did everyone a favor by hauling her home." Okay, if this was a test, I think I passed. They're laughing and I think they assume that Jocelyn and I are not as good of friends as it may have appeared yesterday.

We go into the mall and as we do the shops, I find out these girls aren't that much different from my friends back in Boston. We pretty much like the same kinds of fashion, same designers, same shoes, same brands of cosmetics. We all love sushi, green tea, and are comfortable with Greek food. Really, in some ways, it's a very small world. I find out that Kendra went out with hottie Logan Worthington, but apparently the chemistry wasn't quite right, since they only went out once. Meredith throws a jab at Kendra, suggesting that perhaps Logan wasn't as attracted to her as she was to him, but the icy looks this gets her from both Sally and Kendra shut Meredith up pretty quickly. I suspect they shut her down due to my presence.

A reminder to me that I'm still on the outside. I'm still not welcome in their sacred space or allowed to know all their secrets. And I realize I'm being watched. Every move I make, every word I say, is carefully weighed and scrutinized. But I remain on my best behavior. I try to act relaxed, like I'm cool, but I stay alert. I compliment someone when the timing is right, not laying it on too thick, but sounding sincere—and intelligent. I realize it's important to sound intelligent. It's one of the things that I've learned can really work for me. I am respected for it. As long as I don't go too far. No one likes to be around Miss Smarty Pants. I learned that lesson in fourth grade when I beat my best friend in a mental math contest, then made sure that everyone in the school knew about it. It's better to be quietly intelligent. You don't need to rub anyone's nose in it.

By the time we're done and heading home, I feel exhausted. But I think maybe I passed their test. Or, more accurately, *today's* portion of the test. Who knows how much more is left? But I'm pretty sure it's not over yet. I thank Kendra for inviting me, tell Sally and Meredith that it was fun getting to know them better, and then say that I'll see them on Monday.

"I'll call you," says Kendra, which actually surprises me, but I just nod like that's perfectly normal. And that's when I notice Sally bristle ever so slightly. It's a small gesture, almost unnoticeable. But like a venomous snake that's posing to strike, it's a warning. I remember now that Sally is Kendra's best friend and obviously unhappy with the idea that Kendra's befriending me. According to

Jocelyn, Sally has occupied this enviable position for at least two years, and I'm sure she's not willing to relinquish it now. Especially to a newcomer like me.

Watch your step, I think as I walk toward my front door. Not literally, of course. It's not like I'm going to trip and fall on my face right now. I'm thinking of Sally. Not only is this test not finished, but it could become even tougher now. And I find this very irksome. I mean, just when I think I don't have to be on my lookout for Kendra anymore, I realize Sally could be an even worse threat. When will I get a break?

seven

On Sunday morning my mom announces that she's taking the day off.

"That's cool," I tell her. I want to add, *What else is new?* since she often takes the day off on Sunday—usually to go shopping, her favorite form of stress relief. But I don't say this. She seems to be grumpy enough already. Why push things? Besides, I got to go shopping yesterday. Even if it wasn't exactly stress free.

"So you'll stick around the house then?" she asks as she picks up her new Marc Jacobs bag—the one I've been eyeing lately and wish I could borrow sometime because I'm pretty sure it would impress Kendra. One nice thing about my mom is that she really does have good taste, especially for an older woman, and she doesn't mind spending money on designers either. "You'll keep an eye on Nana?"

"Sure. Have a good time." I point to her purse. "I so love that bag, Mom."

She shakes a finger at me. "You already got my Burberry bag, Reagan. Don't sneak off with this one next."

I laugh. "It was just a compliment, Mom. Have fun, okay?"

She smiles. "Thanks. Maybe I'll get you something while I'm out."

I consider putting in a specific request but think better of it. My mom does not like to be told what to do. Better to just play it safe. "Cool," I say.

I'm actually relieved to spend the day at home without Mom in the house. I'm ready for some R&R. Oh, it's not that I don't love my mom. I totally do. But she can be pretty demanding. And the truth is, it's hard to really relax when she's home. It's like she wants me to stay busy or something. I realize this is because Mom has a type A personality, which she is quick to point out to anyone interested. In fact, everyone who knows my mom is fully aware of this. I've even overheard coworkers talking behind her back. Naturally, I'd never repeat anything like that to Mom. There would be no point.

"Is Diane gone?" asks Nana as she emerges from her room wearing her favorite pink sweats and an old cowboy hat that used to belong to my grandpa.

"Yeah, for the day," I tell her as a form of reassurance. Even though Nana's memory is fading quickly, she seems to know to lay low when her daughter's in a foul mood.

"Do you want to watch . . ." She pauses to think. "That TV . . ." She frowns now, then points to me. "That thing . . ."

"You mean the country music channel on TV?" I ask, knowing full well that's what she means.

She thinks for a moment. "Yes, that's it."

"Sure," I tell her, heading to the family room to turn on the TV. I go to the CMT station, then crank the sound up the way Nana likes it. This is one of Nana's favorite pastimes, and I usually put it on before I go to school in the morning. But whenever Mom is home, we leave it off because Mom can't stand country music. Worse than that, she makes fun of it and anyone who enjoys it. She even teases Nana for liking it. Nana used to say that the only reason she listens to it is because it reminds her of Grandpa. He used to play the steel guitar. I don't exactly remember that about him since I was barely walking when Grandpa died, but I've seen photos of him with his guitar and I imagine that I heard him play.

After Grandpa died, Nana came to live with us. Or maybe we went to live with her. I'm not even sure now which way it was. But I do know that without Nana's help, my mom wouldn't be nearly as financially comfortable as she is now. Not that we're rich like Jocelyn likes to think. But we're okay. It's because of Nana that my mom can afford to go out and buy Marc Jacobs bags.

LeAnn Rimes is on CMT right now. It looks like she has a new video, and I actually stay to watch it. Nana is swaying to the music and I decide to dance too. I would totally die if anyone saw me dancing with Nana to LeAnn Rimes, but it's actually pretty fun. This is one of my biggest secrets. I actually like country music. But there is no way I would tell anyone—not even my old best friend, Geneva—about this. I've liked LeAnn Rimes since I was a little girl. I almost feel like I grew up with her, although she was probably already fairly grown up back then.

"Wasn't that great?" I say to Nana when the song ends.

She's smiling. "Yes. What is her name, Reagan? I can't remember." I tell her and she nods. "Yes. That's it. LeAnn Rimes. LeAnn Rimes."

I stick around and listen to a few more, but then I hear the doorbell and I nearly jump out of my socks.

"Who's there?" asks Nana, almost as if she's playing the part of a knock-knock joke.

I turn down the sound on a video of Clint Black, which I know will disappoint Nana. "I'll go check," I say. "You stay here."

So I make a dash to the door and am horrified to see that it's

Sally. What is she doing here? I take in a calming breath, smooth my hair, then open the door.

"Hi, Reagan," she says, peering past me like she wants to come in and snoop around.

"Sally!" I create a surprised expression for her benefit. "What are you doing here?"

Now she holds out a red and white shoebox. "Somehow your shoes got shipped to my house."

"Huh?" I study the box, then realize they're our new cheerleading shoes. "How do you know they're mine?" I ask somewhat suspiciously. I have a feeling she's just using this to get into my house, maybe to spy on me so she can report to the others. Or maybe I'm just paranoid.

"You're the only one who wears a six." She points to the size on the box. "Right? Did you get your shoes yesterday?"

I shake my head. "Not that I know."

"Then these have to be yours." She cranes her neck slightly, still trying to see inside.

"I'd ask you in," I say quickly. "But my grandmother is here and we're in the middle of something."

"Oh." She nods. "Yeah, okay. See you tomorrow then."

"Yeah. And thanks for dropping these by." I want to ask her why she didn't just bring them to school. Why she didn't save herself the trip. But I think I know the answer. She's out to get me. I just know it.

I shut and lock the door, thinking that was a close one. What if she'd sneaked into my house and seen me dancing to Clint Black with Nana? I see Nana now, in her pink sweats and crumpled cowboy hat, softly rocking to the music—a slow number by Toby Keith—and I realize how hokey it would look to someone like Sally.

How would I ever live something like that down? Okay, I know I'm probably overreacting, but these things can and do happen. I really need to be more careful.

I go around and lock the back door and tilt the wood blinds up just enough so someone wouldn't be able to see in from outside, then finally I turn the music up again for Nana. It's the Dixie Chicks now and, as tempting as it is to stay and rock out, I tell Nana that I need to do homework. She looks disappointed but doesn't protest. Still, there's this look in her eyes and it makes me sad.

"It shouldn't take me too long," I promise. "Then we can do something fun, okay?"

Her eyes light up a little. "Okay."

Sometimes, like now, I feel like a total hypocrite. I didn't really have to leave Nana to do homework. Crazy as it seems, I think she knows this. And yet I can't imagine the humiliation I'd feel if someone like Kendra or Sally were to walk in and see me dancing with her to the Dixie Chicks. Talk about setting yourself up.

I sit down on my bed and slowly exhale. Everything feels so tiring to me. Trying to meet other people's standards . . . pretending to be something I'm not . . . jumping through hoops . . . smiling when I don't feel like it — it's all so exhausting. Besides feeling like a hypocrite, which is bad enough, I am starting to feel sort of lost as well. Like I'm not really sure who I am or where I belong. Sometimes I just wish I could escape the whole thing. I lie down on my bed and long for a break — or maybe just a nice long nap. Then, just as I close my eyes, my cell phone starts to ring. I tell myself to just let it ring, but something inside snaps back to attention and I grab it, answering even before I check my caller ID.

"Hey, Reagan," says a voice I suspect belongs to Jocelyn.

"How are you?" I ask.

"I'm okay now. But I was totally wiped out yesterday. Man, please don't ever let me drink that much again, okay?"

"Yeah, sure. I mean, okay."

"Thanks for getting me home. I can't remember much, but I think I remember that."

"No problem. I'm glad you're feeling better."

"Have you ever had a hangover before?"

I sort of laugh. "No. And I don't plan on it either."

"That's because you're smarter than I am."

"Some people have to learn things the hard way, Jocelyn."

"Well, honestly, I am never doing *that* again. The truth is, I've never really been into the whole drinking thing. I just wanted Kendra to think I was. How did she know that neither of us drinks, Reagan?"

"Trust me," I say, "I didn't tell her."

"Maybe she has ESP."

I laugh. "Yeah, maybe."

"So, do you wanna do something today?"

I consider this. On one hand, it would be fun to hang with her. But on the other hand, I promised Mom I'd stay with Nana today. I think about asking Jocelyn to come over here but decide against it. Jocelyn seems pretty cool, but I don't think I can trust her enough to let her see how it really is here. Nana is unpredictable. She could do anything from two-stepping to Garth Brooks to emerging from the bathroom wearing nothing but a cowboy hat. What if something weird happened and Jocelyn told everyone about it? I couldn't deal with that.

"I would do something today," I tell her, "but my grandmother is here and I promised my mom I'd stay with her."

"Is she sick?"

"Sort of. She can't be left alone."

"I could come over there."

"Nooo," I say slowly. "She's not that comfortable with other people. It's kind of upsetting, you know."

"Oh."

"Sorry."

"No, that's okay. I'm sorry for you. It sounds like a drag being stuck with a sick old grandma. I think I might get my mom to take me to the mall." She laughs. "Not to buy anything, of course, but just to look around and get ideas. I wish you could come."

"Me too," I say. And that's actually true. Just hearing Jocelyn's voice now makes me want to spend time with her. Oh, she might not be a class-A friend, especially after getting drunk at Kendra's party the other night. But she is fun. And in some ways I do think I could trust her. Oh, why is life so complicated?

"See ya tomorrow then?"

"Yeah," I say. "I'll pick you up for school in the morning."

"Thanks!"

I push the End button, then fall back onto my bed. Seriously, I am so tired I feel like I could probably sleep for a couple of hours, but then I hear this loud crash and I leap to my feet and rush out in time to see Nana standing in a mess of broken pottery. And she is barefoot.

"Don't move," I yell at her, which actually makes her jump. "Really, Nana," I say in a calmer voice. "Don't move, okay? You'll cut your feet if you step on any of that." Then I run for the broom and sweep a path for her. I can tell by the brightly colored shards that it's the Mexican bowl, Mom's favorite piece of pottery, that's been broken. I have no idea why Nana had it out. "It's okay," I say as I guide her away from the broken pieces, but she is crying by the time I help her sit down on the couch.

"I'm sorry, Reagan," she sobs.

"It's okay, Nana." I pat her on the shoulder. "I'll clean it up."

"That bowl . . ."

"It's okay, Nana," I say again. "It's just a bowl."

"Diane's bowl."

"Yeah. Why did you have it?"

"Chips. I wanted chips."

I remember now how Mom sometimes uses that bowl for nachos. Of course, to anyone whose mind works in a normal fashion it makes no sense why Nana thought getting that bowl down would magically produce chips. But somehow I understand.

I get the remnants of the bowl swept up and dumped into the trash compactor but worry that Mom will see them there. So I put some newspapers and other things on top to hide them. Of course, she will eventually notice the missing bowl. But no need to tell her on her day off.

"Want to go get some nacho chips?" I ask Nana when I find her sitting on the couch right where I left her.

She smiles and nods.

"Stay there," I say. "I'll get your shoes."

But once we're in my car, I realize I don't really want to take a chance of running into anyone I know. So instead of going to my favorite taco place, which has the best fish tacos in the state, I drive all the way across town, choosing a rundown taco stand I would normally avoid—a place I can be equally sure my peers would avoid. Will the madness ever end?

eight

To my amazement, the first half of the following week goes extremely well. So well that I think maybe I've made it past some invisible social barrier. Maybe I have actually arrived. Kendra is treating me not only like a fellow human, but like a friend. Meredith is also being very nice. Even Sally, although a bit frosty, seems to be trying. The only fly in the ointment is Jocelyn.

"What is going on with you?" she asks me on Wednesday after practice. As usual, I'm giving her a ride home. But her attitude these past couple of days is making me rethink this friendship.

"What do you mean?"

"I mean you and Kendra—when did you two get to be so buddy-buddy?"

"At her party," I say as I turn onto Jocelyn's street. "Oh, that's right, you were too wasted to notice."

"Don't you know she's setting you up?"

"I don't think so." Now, I don't want to overstate my case, but I'm almost certain that Kendra is *not* setting me up. If anything, I think she may be trying to set up Jocelyn. But no way am I going to mention this. Besides, I don't know it for sure. All I know is that Kendra's been saying little things about Jocelyn, behind her back of course, which makes me think that Jocelyn is about to become

Kendra's new target. And, while I do feel bad for Jocelyn, I have to admit I feel some relief at getting a break from this position myself.

"I think you're being pretty naive," says Jocelyn as I pull up in front of her house.

"Whatever." I sigh in a tired way. "I just get so sick of all this, Jocelyn. Isn't it possible we might all just end up being friends?"

She laughs. "I wish. But unfortunately, that's not going to happen. I overheard Kendra making fun of me today. It was in the bathroom at lunch, and she didn't know I was in the stall. Or maybe she did!"

"What did she say?" I ask in a way that sounds like I'm totally bored by all this.

"She said Chad was just using me at the party to have a good time and that he took advantage of me because I was drunk." Jocelyn's voice breaks a little. "She said he won't give me the time of day once he gets what he wants from me."

Now, that's pretty harsh. But I wonder if Jocelyn really heard Kendra right. Or maybe she's blowing it out of proportion.

"Well, that's sort of true," I point out.

"What?" Her eyes flash with indignation.

"I mean it's possible that some guys will take advantage of a girl who gets drunk—can you deny that?"

"Well, no. But I don't think Chad's like that."

"But you've been complaining about how he's barely spoken to you this week."

"Yeah, but don't forget he was a little wasted too. Maybe he's embarrassed."

"Or maybe he was so wasted that he can't remember who he spent the evening with."

"Oh, Reagan!"

"Well, you don't know, Jocelyn. And that's probably what you get from drinking too much."

She opens the car door now. "Thanks for the lecture, Reagan. I really needed that." She shakes her head and frowns. "And I thought you were my friend."

I sigh. "I am your friend. But friends don't let friends act stupid."

"Thanks." Then she slams the door and I drive away. Okay, I'm thinking maybe it's about time to cut this girl loose. The way things are developing with Kendra, I might do just fine without Miss Loose Cannon anyway.

When I get home, I notice that the front door is standing open and suddenly feel alarmed. Is it possible that Nana has wandered out? Is she fully dressed? Could she be wandering around lost? I quickly pull my car into the garage. As usual, Mom's not home yet, which is a relief. She's been hinting again that our setup with Nana is not working. And part of me thinks maybe she's right.

I hurry into the house. "Nana?" I yell loudly. "Nana?"

"She's in here," calls a female voice from the direction of the bathroom. Okay, now I'm really worried. Is some stranger in our house? In the bathroom with Nana? I run toward the bathroom, then notice muddy footprints leading from the front door to here—is it possible that we had a break-in? I wonder if I should grab the phone.

"We're in the bathroom," calls the voice. And now it sounds a little familiar and not at all threatening.

"What is going on?" I demand as I push open the partially closed door in time to see Nana with her yellow sweatpants hiked up to her knees as she sits on a kitchen chair that's situated next to the bathtub.

"Hey, Reagan," says Andrea Lynch, my temporary class-C

summertime friend. She looks up from where she's bent over, washing what looks like a whole lot of mud from Nana's feet. The bottom of the bathtub is brown.

"Hi, Reagan," says Nana with a happy smile. "I got dirty."

"I found her in my mom's garden," says Andrea as she rubs some soap into a blue washcloth.

"I wanted tomatoes," explains Nana.

"Yeah." Andrea rubs the soapy washcloth over Nana's twisted old foot, then uses the European shower nozzle to spray it off until it's almost clean. "Of course, the tomatoes are gone by now. But she was walking around in the garden without shoes and when I asked her if she needed help, she said she couldn't remember where she lived."

"I forget things." Nana shakes her head sadly.

"So I walked her home and then I asked if she needed help getting her feet cleaned."

"She's a good foot washer," says Nana proudly. "What's your name, girl?"

"Andrea," I offer.

Andrea tosses me a look. "Oh, you do remember my name?"

I sort of roll my eyes. "Yeah."

"Well, I didn't know how to get her into the house without making a mess. The front door was the only one open. Sorry that the floors got a little muddy."

"That's okay," I tell her. "If you have things under control here, I'll go clean up the rest before my mom gets home."

"That's cool."

"That's cool," echoes Nana, sounding like an elderly teenager.

As I get out the mop and start working on the hardwood floors, I can hear the two of them in the bathroom just chatting away like they're old friends. I don't catch everything they say, but I can tell that Andrea is completely comfortable with Nana. And, judging by the way Nana's talking, I can tell that she likes and trusts Andrea.

We finish up about the same time. Just as I'm pouring the bucket of dirty mop water out, Andrea and Nana come into the kitchen. Nana has on a big smile and her nonskid moccasin slippers.

"Andrea put lotion on my feet," says Nana proudly.

"Good for Andrea," I say in a less than friendly tone.

"Be nice," says Nana.

I blink and look at Nana, surprised that she picked up on that. "I'll go clean up the bathroom," I say, wanting an escape from this strange pair.

"I already did," says Andrea.

"Oh."

"I told Andrea that we could have cookies and milk," says Nana.

"We don't—"

"That's okay," says Andrea quickly. She gives me a wary glance. "I have to go now." And before I can say anything, she takes off.

"My friend," says Nana sadly. "You weren't nice to my friend, Reagan."

"Sorry," I say. And the truth is, I really am. Still, I don't know what to do about it. Why is everything so complicated?

***

The next day things get even more complicated when Sally asks Falon about the annual fall barbecue. "Isn't it about time we started talking about it?"

Falon just holds up her hands. "You can talk about it all you want, but I really don't care whether or not we have—"

"We always have it," protests Meredith. "It's a tradition. It's our time to bond together."

"That's right," says Sally. "We need to set the date."

"Fine," says Falon. "Set the date. But hurry up, okay? We need to get practicing."

"Next week is homecoming," says Meredith. "How about the Saturday after that?" Fortunately everyone agrees. Even Kendra, although she's been uncharacteristically quiet today.

"But where will we have it?" asks Sally. She looks over at Kendra as if she expects her to help out now.

Kendra shrugs. "Well, if I wasn't just an alternate cheerleader, I'd offer to have it at my place. But in this case, I guess I won't."

Some of the girls groan in disappointment.

"That's too bad," I say, hoping to show some support for Kendra, and she smiles gratefully.

"Why don't you have it then?" says Sally suddenly.

"Oh, I don't think—"

"Yeah," says Meredith. "We should let one of the new girls host the barbecue." She glances at the others and they all quickly agree.

"Sort of an initiation," teases Meredith.

"I don't think I want to host—"

"Then Jocelyn can do it," says Sally.

"No way!" demands Jocelyn.

"Okay. Then, Reagan, you're on," proclaims Sally. "All in favor, say aye." And before I can protest, everyone, including Jocelyn (little traitor) yells, "Aye!"

I feel like I'm going to faint or maybe throw up. How on earth am I supposed to host the barbecue at my house? I think about Nana and the crazy things she's done already this week. Or what about my mom and her tendency to go ballistic if anyone makes a mess? How can I possibly pull this off with those things to contend with? Still, it seems useless to argue, and besides, Falon is yelling at us to get in line for a new cheer. I decide to approach Falon after practice. I'll beg her to get me off the hook. If that doesn't work, I'll go to Coach Anderson. And if that doesn't work . . . well, maybe I'll just quit. I mean, seriously, it's just not worth the torture.

I see Kendra off to the left as we practice. As usual, she's not actually in the lineup, but I suddenly wonder if this is her big setup. Did Kendra get Sally to do this so I would be stuck hosting the stupid barbecue and get so intimidated that I'd quit cheerleading and she'd get to be back on? No, that seems impossible. For one thing, no one—well, besides Andrea—has any idea what kind of madness lives at my house. For another thing, it would've made much more sense to target Jocelyn, since by now I'm sure that someone on this squad must know her financial status and that she lives in a cruddy little house and would be too embarrassed to have the barbecue. In fact, I reassure myself, if all else fails, maybe I can influence Kendra to influence Sally to push this whole thing onto Jocelyn. The way she's been acting today—all offended at me for practically nothing—almost makes me wish this on her.

"Falon," I say as we're walking back to the locker room after practice, "I cannot host the barbecue at my—"

"I don't really care, Reagan." She turns and gives me a warning look. "The barbecue doesn't really have anything to do with the squad. For all I care, we can just forget it. Tell them you don't want to have it and—"

"They'll get mad at me."

She shakes her head. "Like I said, I don't care. And to be honest, I'm sick to death of the bickering and game playing. It almost makes me want to quit." She glances over to where Kendra and several others are huddled together, talking. "But I wouldn't give her the satisfaction." Then Falon walks off.

Great. I consider approaching Coach Anderson, but I have a feeling she'd back Falon. And I suppose I don't blame her. Except that this just is not fair. I look over to where Kendra and the others are still standing, and I suspect they're talking about me now. I cannot let this go on. I've made such progress with Kendra these past few days and I'm not about to lose it now.

I join them and the talking stops.

"Hey, Reagan," says Kendra. "What's up?"

"Well, this is the deal," I begin. "I really don't want to host the barbecue."

Kendra frowns and looks sincerely disappointed in me. "Why not? It's really fun, Reagan."

"Fun for you, maybe. But from what I've heard, you've set the standard pretty high and I know there's no way I can do a barbecue that will be even one-tenth as nice."

"Oh, Reagan." She puts her arm around my shoulders. "You're so sweet."

"Really, Kendra," I insist, "it's too intimidating. I can't do it. You're a hard act to follow."

"Isn't she sweet?" Kendra says to the others, and to my amazement, they all agree. Well, except for Sally. I can tell she's not buying it.

"Why don't you make Jocelyn do it?" suggests Kendra.

"Yeah," says Meredith. "She's the youngest. Let's *make* her do it."

The next thing I know — feeling like I just jumped onto a moving train — we are approaching Jocelyn. She's already stripped down, wrapping a towel around her, and about to head for the showers. When she sees us coming, she looks scared.

"We decided you get to host the barbecue," announces Meredith.

"We voted and it was unanimous."

Okay, I realize that's not completely true. But it's not my job to set anyone straight. I keep my mouth shut, telling myself I'm only a spectator here.

"No way!" yells Jocelyn.

"Way!" Sally yells back and it turns into a shouting match. And cheerleaders are good at yelling. If Coach Anderson was anywhere to be seen, I'm sure she'd shut them up. I see Falon over by her locker. I can tell she's listening, but she doesn't interfere. I'm not sure if this is a tactic on her part or if she's afraid. I know I wouldn't want to get in the middle of this.

I can tell that Jocelyn is on the verge of tears when she finally backs down. She really didn't have a chance—she should've recognized that from the start. I mean, Jocelyn might be loud and have a temper, but she's no match for these girls. She narrows her eyes and cuts loose with some surprisingly foul language. I hope Falon isn't close enough to hear, since this is a serious infraction of the cheerleaders' contract—but then, so was that drinking party last week. Furious, but undeniably defeated, Jocelyn stomps off to the showers and stays there for a long time. And although I feel sorry for her and I have no idea how she's going to handle this barbecue challenge, I also feel extremely relieved. Like I missed a bullet. Unfortunately my relief is tinged with some serious guilt. I am not proud of myself.

nine

"YOU'RE A PIECE OF WORK, REAGAN," SAYS JOCELYN ONCE WE'RE IN MY CAR. They're the first words she's spoken since the big argument. And I know her silent treatment was aimed at me, since all the other cheerleaders had long since left the locker room by the time Jocelyn emerged from the showers. I expected her to be a shriveled prune.

"I'm sorry," I tell her as I put my car into reverse. "But it wasn't really my fault."

"Uh-huh."

I can tell she doesn't believe me. To be fair, I don't believe me either. "Honestly, Jocelyn," I try. "All I said was that I couldn't host the barbecue and suddenly they were all like, 'Let's make Jocelyn do it,' and—"

"And you didn't stand up for me. You didn't defend me. I thought you were my friend."

"Just because I'm your friend doesn't mean I have to fight your battles, Jocelyn." Suddenly I'm angry. I mean, she's not the only one with crud to deal with. Sure, she might be poor. But maybe being poor is better than living with an angry mom and a crazy grandma, not to mention being the new girl. She's not saying anything now. I think she's pouting, but I'm getting really mad. "And what about you?" I toss back. "I thought you were my friend, but just how are you doing that anyway? I'm the one who gives you rides everywhere. I'm the one who helped you when you got plastered at Kendra's party. What kind of friend are you being to me, Jocelyn?"

Now there's a great long silence and I think she's crying, but I'm so angry that I don't really care. I mean, really, why does she get to pick on me for being a lousy friend when she's really not doing much better? What's fair about that?

Finally I'm pulling up to her house and she's opening the door and I think, *Fine, just leave without saying anything—I am finished with you!*

"I'm sorry," she mutters. "You're right. I haven't been a good friend. I'm sorry!" Then she shuts the door and runs up to her house. Great, now I can't even stay mad at her.

When I get to my house, I feel like hitting something, and I know all I have to look forward to is cleaning up Nana's messes before Mom gets home. But to my surprise there are no messes. And Nana looks neat and clean and fully dressed as she sits in her recliner watching the country music channel.

"Hi, Nana," I say cautiously. "What's going on?"

She looks up and smiles. "Nothing."

I walk through the kitchen. All is clean and tidy. I go to the downstairs bathroom—the same. Even her bedroom is respectable. I come out and stand between her and the TV, which makes her frown. "Did you clean house?" I ask, thinking maybe it's a miracle. Maybe whatever it is that's been making her act so strangely the past couple of years has moved on.

"No," she says with a grin. "My friend was here."

"Your friend?"

She gets a puzzled look. "That girl . . . the one I found in the garden."

"Andrea?"

She points a finger in the air. "Yes! Andrea. She came to see me again today."

"Oh." I move out of the way of the TV, go into the kitchen, and start poking around to see what I can fix for dinner. What is Andrea up to anyway? Does she think if she's nice to Nana, I will suddenly want to be her friend? No one could be that crazy. I finally decide on spaghetti, shoving thoughts of both Andrea and Jocelyn from my mind.

**

The next morning I don't know what to do. Normally I give Jocelyn a ride to school, but I feel like our friendship is over and I don't really want to go pick her up and prolong something that needs to end. I consider calling her and making some excuse, but then I come up with an easier way out. I decide to be late to school. When I don't show up, she'll have to walk. I know this is mean and she'll be late for class. But then, so will I. Doesn't that balance things out?

I take my time fixing Nana's breakfast. I take even more time fixing her lunch—tuna salad, which she loves. I even go ahead and change her sheets, a chore I usually put off for the end of the day. And I put a load of laundry in the washer and really scrub down the kitchen. I pause to admire our kitchen. It really is pretty cool, especially compared to our seventies condo back in Boston. I couldn't believe it when I first saw this house. Everything was new and clean. The kitchen, with its dark cherry cabinets, granite slab countertops, and stainless-steel appliances, looked like something right out of a magazine. And we'd never had hardwood floors before. I think they look really elegant, and Mom plans to get an oriental rug for the entryway. Seriously, if it wasn't for the Nana factor, I'd probably consider hosting a barbecue here just to help Jocelyn off the hook. Although it wouldn't be as uptown as Kendra's, I think I might possibly be able to pull it off with a certain amount of class.

But as I walk through the living room, where Nana is already seated in her pink electric-lift recliner, I reconsider. There's no way I will offer to have the barbecue here. I feel sorry for Jocelyn, but she'll have to fend for herself. Fortunately Nana has no sense of time and has no idea that I'm running late or even that it's a school day. My plan is to miss all of first period, which is AP History, but I'm totally caught up so I'm not worried. If anyone asks, I'll tell them I had a flat tire. In fact, that's what I'll tell Jocelyn too. Of course, she'll ask why I didn't call. I glance at my cell phone, still turned off and sitting on the breakfast bar. I'll tell her my battery was dead. That's easy enough.

"Bye, Nana," I say as I sling my new Marc Jacobs bag over my shoulder. Mom's actually letting me use this one since she got a Kate Spade pocketbook that's to die for. (I'll figure out a way to borrow that later.)

"Bye-bye, honey." Nana wiggles her fingers in a wave, then turns back to watch the Martina McBride video.

I get to school in time for second period, and for the rest of the day I avoid Jocelyn. Fortunately I only see her once and that's as I'm coming into the cafeteria. She's sitting with the JV cheerleaders, and I'm thinking that's probably a good thing. I sit with Kendra and her friends during lunch. It's amazing how easy it is now. It's like they're really accepting me. But that's where I hear the news.

"Jocelyn bailed on the barbecue," says Meredith.

"I heard that," says Kendra, shaking her head as if she's disappointed.

"I *knew* she would," says Sally in a vicious tone. "She's such a baby. They shouldn't let sophomores try out for varsity. It's just wrong."

Then they all go on about how girls should have to be at least juniors to be on varsity, and how it's really Jocelyn's fault that Kendra is still left out.

"But how did Jocelyn get out of it?" I finally ask. Okay, I'm curious to find out how Jocelyn escaped this horrible fate just in case they decide to force it back on me now.

"Didn't you hear?" asks Kendra.

I shake my head.

"Her mother wrote a note."

They all laugh as if this is hysterically funny.

"How lame is that?"

"Totally pathetic."

"Poor Jocelyn," says Kendra. "I think the stress may be getting to her."

I nod and act like I'm with them. But at the same time, I'm thinking the stress is getting to me.

"Anyway . . ." Sally looks at me and I know something is up. "We've decided that you should go ahead and host the barbecue, Reagan. Are you okay with that?" She actually smiles at me like we're good friends now.

"And I'll help you with the details," announces Kendra. "I won't be coming, of course, since I'm only an alternate. But you're my friend, Reagan, and I can help you figure things out. Okay?"

"I . . . uh . . . I don't know . . ."

"Come on," says Meredith. "You'll be fine. I saw your house and it's brand-new and way nicer than mine." She jabs Sally with her elbow. "And yours too, if you don't mind me saying so."

"But, I—"

"We'll go shopping together," promises Kendra. "I know this totally great party store where we can get some really cool plates and napkins and things. If you want I'll even call my caterer and you can—"

"Okay!" I say suddenly, surprising even myself. "I'll do it."

Sally looks shocked, like she was really hoping that I'd refuse and make everyone mad, putting me, like Jocelyn, on the outside again. But I won't give her the pleasure.

"Good girl," says Kendra. "And you'll see, entertaining can be fun. You just need to learn the tricks."

I nod. "Yeah, you're probably right, Kendra."

"By the way, Reagan, I totally adore your bag. Marc Jacobs?"

As I confirm this and we all gush about how much we love Marc Jacobs shoes as well as bags, I can't help but notice the grim expression on Sally's face. And somehow that makes everything worthwhile. I can tell she's furious about (1) the fact that I stood up to the barbecue challenge and (2) Kendra's offer to help me make it a success. She is totally jealous that Kendra is giving me all this attention. Well, tough.

Once again, when I get home from school, things are nice and neat. I ask Nana if her friend visited again today and she smiles and says yes. And, while I don't want to think too hard about why Andrea is doing this, I do feel grateful for the poor girl. Still, I don't think I actually owe her anything since I never asked for her to do any of this. And she doesn't have to unless she wants to.

Besides, I don't have time to think about those things now since I'm obsessing over how I will possibly pull off this barbecue in just eight days. The biggest part of the challenge is what to do about Nana. Then it occurs to me that I might be able to hire Andrea to Nana-sit at her house. Maybe I could take Nana over that morning to give me enough time to get things in order. And I could move the horrible recliner into Nana's bedroom and lock the door to make sure no one goes in. Okay, it seems like a lot of work, but it's necessary. And I think it's doable.

Hopefully Andrea will be up for this. I mean, it's not like she has a life or anything. And, as I recall, it seems like her parents aren't too well off, so she'd probably be glad to make some extra money. Even so, I decide to wait for just the right moment to ask her. I'll probably need to be a little bit nicer to her first. But I need to be careful how I do this, because I really don't want her to get the idea that someone like me needs someone like her. Because I don't.

Our new uniforms arrive in time for the game. Everyone is so excited to try them on that we decide to use the first part of class to make sure the right items came and that they all fit.

"Here's yours, Reagan," says Sally, thrusting a plastic-wrapped package at me. Kendra is standing next to her, almost as if she's supervising. But when I look down I notice a white computer label with the name Jocelyn Matthews printed on it. I'm about to mention this when Kendra reaches down and rips off the sticker. "Just a mistake," she says, shaking her head. "Don't worry about it. Jocelyn's already got her uniform."

Even so, I double-check the size of the top, and it's what I ordered. When I slip it on, it's perfect. Soon I've got the whole outfit on. And when my turn comes to look in the mirror, since the bathroom's crowded with cheerleaders now, I can see that I actually look pretty good in it. Really, I think royal blue and white look much better on me than my old cheerleading outfit of brown and gold. I wonder if I should put my hair in a pony or just let it hang loose . . .

"What the—" Jocelyn is holding up a uniform now, high so that we can all see, and I must say it looks rather enormous. "Whose is

103

this?" she demands, looking at the rest of us with suspicious eyes.

"Planning to put on some weight, are you?" teases Meredith.

"This is *not* what I ordered!" she exclaims.

"Well, it had *your* name on it," says Sally.

"Where?" demands Jocelyn. "I didn't see my name on it anywhere."

"On the sticker," says Sally. "It was right on the front of the package. It must've fallen off."

"Whatever," snaps Jocelyn. "The point is, it does *not* fit me. It's like size *elephant*, and there's no way I can wear it." She slips the huge top over her head to make her point and we all laugh, because it looks like a maternity smock.

"That's too bad," says Meredith.

"Too bad for you," says Jocelyn. "Now we'll all have to wear our old uniforms tonight."

"No, we won't," says Sally calmly, but in a cold voice. "It's not *our* fault if you don't know how to write down your correct size, Jocelyn. Maybe the coach helped you with those things back on JV, but this is varsity, honey. We expect you to grow up here."

Jocelyn lets out a low growling sound. "This is not fair."

Meredith shakes her head. "You're right about that, Jocelyn. It's *not* fair to us that you screwed up. Now we'll only have seven girls in uniform tonight. I wonder what Falon's going to say."

Jocelyn looks nervous now. She glances over at where Kendra is standing. Kendra, like the rest of us, is trying on her uniform, the one she insisted on getting just in case we needed an alternate. "I can borrow Kendra's," says Jocelyn in an amazingly confident voice.

"What?" says Kendra, clearly surprised.

"I said, I'll borrow *your* uniform," says Jocelyn. "You don't need it. Sure, it'll be a little baggy, but I can use safety pins to—"

"No way. You are *not* going to use safety pins to poke holes into my uniform," says Kendra in a calm tone. "Not unless you plan to pay for it."

"I only want to borrow it," says Jocelyn, less confident now. "Just for the night."

"You don't have to borrow it," says Kendra as if she's giving in. "You can buy it from me, and then you can safety pin it to your little heart's content. You're going to have to buy a new uniform anyway."

Jocelyn looks surprised by this. "Why?"

"You know they're nonreturnable," says Meredith. "It's not like they can resell a Belmont Cougars uniform in, like, size 50 to anyone else. You're stuck with it, sweetie."

"But I —"

"Maybe you can get it altered," I say, feeling sorry for poor Jocelyn.

"Yeah, you've got plenty of fabric to work with," says Sally.

"You could probably upholster a couch with the leftover fabric," teases Meredith.

Jocelyn looks totally crushed now. I know she can't afford to buy another uniform. It took almost all her money to pay for this. And I am haunted by the image of Kendra ripping that label off of my package. But this reminds me of something. At my other high school, our uniforms always came with our embroidered name emblems already attached. These have the Cougars emblems, but not our names.

"Where are our name emblems?" I ask Sally.

"Oh, they came separately this time," she says quickly.

"Why?" I ask.

"Because it was a rush order," she says. "The name tags actually got here a couple of days ago. I think Coach Anderson has them in her office. By the way, this means we all have to sew them on ourselves. Or if you're like Jocelyn, you might try safety pins." She laughs.

"How's it going in here?" asks Falon. She comes into the bathroom wearing her uniform, her name emblem already neatly attached. Miss Perfect, I'm thinking it should read. "Did everything come? Do they fit okay?"

"Everyone's except for Jocelyn's," says Sally. "She seems to be numerically challenged. Instead of a size 2 she must've hit the computer key twice and ordered a 22."

Everyone laughs, but Falon only frowns as she studies Jocelyn's oversized uniform. "This is a total disaster." She turns to the rest of us. "So what's the plan? What are we going to do about it?"

"I offered to sell her my uniform," says Kendra. "It would need to be taken in a little, but it's — "

"That's a great idea!" Falon looks clearly relieved. "Thanks, Kendra." She turns to Jocelyn. "You okay with that?"

"Fine!" snaps Jocelyn. "If it makes everyone happy, I'll buy it from her."

Kendra looks a little surprised by this announcement, but she just nods. "Okay. I'll go take it off and you can try it on. The skirt might actually fit you because it's a size 4 and you look like you're bigger on the bottom." Then Kendra sticks out her chest. "Of course, you won't fill out the top nearly as well as I do." Then she laughs.

Jocelyn looks like she's about to snarl or hit someone, but she controls herself. "Thanks a lot, Kendra. I'll have to pay you later."

Kendra smiles. "No problem. I'm sure you're good for it."

Now, I'm not so sure about this, but I keep my mouth shut as I check out my own uniform, which seems to fit just fine. I decide not to check the size. I don't think I really want to know.

Okay, the truth is, I'm not entirely sure what just transpired in here or who's actually to blame for this craziness. I do, however, know that something is up and that both Sally and Kendra are involved. But I also know that I could be considered an accessory to the crime—if you could call it a crime, which seems a bit extreme. And I also know that I filled out my order form perfectly and that I put down the correct size. I'm pretty much a straight size 2 when it comes to uniforms. But Sally was the one who sent in the order, so if anyone tampered with anything, it was probably her. The question is, did she mess with my order or Jocelyn's? I think I know the answer. But I do wonder how much Kendra was involved at the time. Even so, I have to ask myself, *Does it really matter?* I decide to think about it later.

The most important thing at the moment, I tell myself as we start practicing the fight song, is to get it together in time for tonight's game. We are, after all, cheerleaders. And our job is to promote school spirit and enthusiasm and good will. Right? As long as we all have the correct colors and emblems and have our wits about us, is it really that big a deal whose uniform we're wearing?

ten

TONIGHT'S GAME IS TOTALLY DIFFERENT FROM LAST WEEK'S. FOR ONE THING, we have our new uniforms, which I think look really awesome. Even Jocelyn looks just fine wearing Kendra's. After practice today, Kendra informed Jocelyn that she wasn't to do any alterations or safety pinning until she paid for it, so the top's just a little loose, but not so that anyone would really notice. But the other thing that's different about tonight's game is that the chill factor is gone. Well, almost. I suppose some of the girls are still giving Jocelyn the cold shoulder. I've gone out of my way to be nice to her—although she's actually been freezing me out.

"Why do you even bother with her?" Meredith asks me at halftime.

"Huh?" I play dumb.

"I mean *Jocelyn*. Why do you keep catering to her? She's acting like a baby tonight, like it's everyone's fault she ordered the wrong size. Just ignore her and maybe she'll straighten up."

I nod like I plan on taking this advice. And maybe I will. Still, I feel guilty and have actually been toying with the idea of offering to split the cost of replacing the gigantic uniform—or maybe just the alteration expense. The problem is, that will probably make her suspicious. And she's already treating me like the

109

enemy. Maybe I should just give it right back to her.

"Hey, Reagan," says Kendra as she hands me a soda. "Looking great out there, girl."

"Thanks," I tell her, surprised at this unexpected kindness. "I just wish you were out here too." I glance at Jocelyn over on the sidelines by herself. It looks like she's pouting again and I'm really fed up with her attitude. "You'd be a whole lot better than some people whose names I won't mention."

Kendra laughs. "I've been hearing that from a lot of people tonight."

"Too bad we can't have a recall election," says Meredith. She and Sally have just joined us. Not wanting to seem selfish, I share sips of my soda with them.

"Now, there's a thought," says Sally. "A recall."

"Oh, there might be easier ways," says Kendra as she looks at Jocelyn. But now the pep band is starting a song and Falon is clapping her hands and it's time to line up for our halftime dance routine.

I try not to think about what Kendra's easier ways might be. But I do feel certain that Kendra won't do anything too mean. After all, she cares about her reputation too. And we all know that Jocelyn isn't exactly the sort of person who will keep her mouth shut when she suffers an injustice. It's actually sort of ironic that Jocelyn is the target now, instead of me. In some ways, I would've been easier to take out because I probably would've gone quietly. I may be a fighter, but I don't really like making scenes or being embarrassed. If Kendra and her friends had kept it up long and hard enough, I would've eventually just given up. It wouldn't have been worth it.

We win this game too, which isn't a huge surprise since this team isn't the best. But we now have two wins, no losses—a perfect record. And everyone is cheering wildly. We're all hugging. I do several handsprings and then we go into our victory yell. I feel so happy—like this is what it's supposed to be like. Everyone in good spirits, everyone having fun. Well, almost everyone. Old sourpuss is still sporting an attitude. I feel like giving Jocelyn a piece of my mind, then think, *Why bother?*

"Hey, Sally," calls Chad, "where's the big celebration gonna be?" Sally and Chad have been pretty chummy tonight. In fact, it seems they've been pretty chummy all week, which is interesting since I don't recall Sally giving that boy the time of day before he and Jocelyn sort of hit it off last weekend. We're picking up our pompoms and things and shoving them into our duffle bags. Jocelyn already has her stuff packed, but she's standing off to one side just watching. Her expression is a mix of sadness and anger. I consider offering her a ride home, but I figure she got here on her own somehow. She can probably get back just fine too. Besides, it's a home game and she doesn't live that far from the school. And if I offer her a ride, I might be stuck with her for the evening. That's not something I'd particularly enjoy.

"Kendra said pizza," says Sally. "Giovanni's, I think."

"Cool," says Chad. "Need a ride?"

Now Sally glances over at Jocelyn like she wants to make sure she can see this. "Sure, Chad." She pecks him on the cheek. "Thanks!"

He looks slightly surprised, then grins.

Now, I know Sally well enough to know that Chad isn't even in her league. For one thing—and it's a biggie—he's a junior and she's a senior. But besides that, he's not even her type. I know this for a fact because I've heard her describe her type. She goes for athletic guys, but blond and quiet. Chad has brown hair and a loud, slightly goofy disposition. So it seems pretty obvious to me (and probably everyone except Chad) that Sally is just using him to hurt Jocelyn. And this makes me mad. In fact, it makes me so mad that I go over and offer Jocelyn a ride.

She narrows her eyes and studies me. "Why?"

I shrug. "Why not? Do you need a ride or don't you?"

"Okay." But her voice is reluctant and this ticks me off. I mean, here I am, going out of my way to be nice to her, and she still acts like a brat. I wish I hadn't bothered. Not only that, but I see Kendra watching me now. I smile at her and sort of shrug, like, *I can't help myself, I feel sorry for this child.* And she smiles back.

"I'm sorry," says Jocelyn as we walk across the parking lot.

"For what?"

"For acting like this."

"Like what?" Playing stupid just seems to work for me.

"You know, all mad. Pouting. Hating everyone."

"Well, you've had a bad day," I say as we get into the car. "I can't really blame you."

Jocelyn sinks into the seat and lets out a sad little sigh. "I don't see why they have to be so mean, Reagan."

I just shrug and start the engine.

"Is it just because I'm the youngest, do you think?"

"I think it's just the way girls are sometimes."

"Well, I can't stand it."

I turn and look at her. "Are you going to quit?"

"No way!"

"Oh."

"Do you want me to quit? Is Kendra controlling you too now? Has she turned you against me too?"

"No, of course not. No one is controlling me but me."

"Yeah, right."

I start driving toward her neighborhood, thinking I cannot wait to drop her off.

"Aren't you going to Giovanni's?" she asks suddenly.

"Huh?"

"I mean, you're going the wrong way."

I take in a quick breath. "Oh, you mean you want to go to Giovanni's too?"

"That's where the celebration is, right?"

"Yeah."

"Well, do you suppose it's okay if I come? I mean, after all, I am still a cheerleader, right? Do you think anyone will mind if I show up? It's a public place, isn't it? Or do I need a special engraved invitation?"

"Of course it's okay if you come, Jocelyn. But maybe you should start acting like a cheerleader." I turn on the next street, start heading the opposite direction.

"Like I should start being really mean? Like I should lie and cheat and try to hurt people?"

"Nooo," I say slowly. "I mean you should be a little more *cheer*ful. You know, *cheer*leader, *cheer*ful, good *cheer*. You should quit going around looking like you're sucking on a lemon."

"Will that make you happy?"

I sigh. What's the use?

"Sorry," she says. "Okay, I promise to try to be nice—full of good cheer."

And by the time we get there, she really seems to be trying. In fact, she puts on a pretty good show that I'm sure surprises everyone. She even flirts with Chad.

"Why did you bring *her*?" asks Kendra.

We're the only ones in the bathroom now. We're both reapplying lip gloss in front of the mirror.

"I couldn't help it," I say. "I was about to take her home and she practically begged me to. It was pathetic really."

"That is sad."

"But I told her if she came she had to be nice."

Kendra laughs. "Oh, she's being nice all right. At least to Chad. I can't remember the last time I saw such shameless flirting. Talk about desperate."

"Sally doesn't really like him, does she?"

"Of course not. She's just trying to get Jocelyn."

"I didn't really think Chad was her type."

"Duh."

Okay, that's a bit of a slam. Time to change the subject. "I saw Logan watching you tonight."

"What?" She looks at me with renewed interest.

I nod and put my lip gloss back into my Marc Jacobs bag. "While you were waiting for drinks. He was just a few feet away from you and it was like he couldn't take his eyes off you." This is partially true, although I'm not sure it's worth much, because the look in his eyes wasn't exactly adoration. More like lust, I think. Like he was just checking out her body, which is not really the way I would want a guy to look at me. But then I know that Kendra still sort of likes him and I think she wants a second chance with him. Maybe I can help facilitate that.

"Really?" She looks amused. "You saw that?"

"And I don't know why he wouldn't be looking," I continue. "You look really great tonight, Kendra. Your outfit is awesome."

She tells me who the designers are and that she just got it last night. "It's hard not being a cheerleader anymore," she says sadly. "But I try to make up for it by looking really good."

"Well, you make our cheerleading outfits look pretty juvenile," I admit.

"Hey, I think the outfits are cute," she says. "I just wish I could have mine back."

"I know."

"But back to Logan. You really think he was watching me?"

I nod. "What's he like anyway? I mean, he's in a couple of my AP classes, but I haven't really talked to him that much. Although he's always nice enough to me."

"Really? You guys are in AP together?"

"Yeah. He seems like a pretty smart guy." Okay, that's a lie. The truth is, I've wondered how he got into the AP classes. Maybe he knows someone.

"Yeah, he is smart. And he's fun too. Hey, maybe you could talk to him sometime for me, Reagan. Just casually, you know. Don't let him know that I asked, but just find out why it hasn't worked out with me."

"Sure. I can do that."

"You're such a good friend." She gives me a little sideways hug and we go back out into the noisy restaurant.

"I thought you guys totally took off," says Sally when we rejoin them at the table. "Where were you?"

"Just in the ladies' room," says Kendra lightly.

"Was someone sick?" Sally looks suspiciously at me.

"No." Kendra sounds impatient. "Just girl talk."

Sally scowls now. "And you left me out?"

"Hey, it's not like we planned some special meeting." Kendra shakes her head. "Lighten up, Sally." Then she nods over to where Jocelyn and Chad are playing a video game. "I thought you were on top of that."

"A girl can only do so much." Sally glares at me now. "Why'd you bring her here anyway?"

"Don't be blaming Reagan for what you can't do," says Kendra in a sharp tone.

Sally slams her drink down on the table, stands up, and walks off. Kendra just shrugs like it's no big deal, like Sally will get over it. But I'm thinking there is trouble in paradise. And this makes me happy.

"Do you want to go to the mall tomorrow?" she asks.

"Sure."

"And we can pick up some party things for the barbecue."

"Sounds great."

Of course, this reminds me that I haven't made arrangements for Nana yet. I did ask Mom if it was okay to host the event at our house next Saturday, and after I convinced her that I would take care of absolutely everything—including Nana—she agreed. Now I just need to talk to Andrea. It's so ironic that I actually have to ask this particular girl for a favor of this magnitude. I'm guessing there will be some groveling to do.

eleven

THE NEXT MORNING AFTER I TAKE CARE OF NANA, I DECIDE TO WALK OVER TO Andrea's house. Somehow I think this might work better if I grovel in person. It's after ten so I assume she'll be up, but I still feel a little awkward as I knock on the door.

"Oh, hello, Reagan," says Mrs. Lynch. "We haven't seen you in ages. How are you anyway?"

"Oh, I've been pretty busy," I tell her. "There's been a lot to get used to with the new school and taking care of my grandmother and all." I throw in that last bit hoping to buy some sympathy, just in case she's not happy about the way I dumped her daughter as a friend a few weeks ago.

She nods. "Yes, I know. Andrea has told us about her. Is it Alzheimer's?"

"I guess so. That's what my mom thinks. She wants to put her in a nursing home. But I'm trying to help out so she can stay with us."

"That's very thoughtful of you."

"Uh, is Andrea here?"

Mrs. Lynch laughs. "Of course. I guess you didn't come over here to visit me, did you?"

"It's nice visiting with you," I say quickly, feeling like a little hypocrite.

"Come on in, make yourself at home. I'll get her."

So I sit on the big plaid sectional in the family room. The layout of this room is just like ours with the fireplace on one end and French doors to the right. Of course, our furniture is nicer. Theirs is pretty frumpy and worn. Andrea says it's because of all her older brothers and sisters before her. She's the youngest of five kids and the only one at home now.

"Hi, Reagan," she says as she joins me in the family room. Her brow is creased in that way I used to warn her would make her wrinkle prematurely. Not that she ever seemed to care. "What's up?"

I begin my rehearsed speech. "I just wanted to thank you for how you've been visiting and helping out with my grandma."

"Oh, that's okay. I think she's fun."

I smile but I'm thinking, *This is so pathetic*—a sixteen-year-old girl befriends a senile old woman and thinks it's fun. I mean, sure, *I* think Nana is fun, but she's *my* grandma. That's totally different. "Well, she really likes you, Andrea. And because cheerleading practice doesn't usually end until after four, well, it really helps break up her day when you stop by. I appreciate it too."

Andrea nods. "Well, that's nice of you to say. By the way, congratulations on making cheerleader. That was pretty amazing."

"Thanks. It's been kind of a challenge, you know." Okay, really, how would she possibly know? Still, I'm trying to be nice here.

"I know," she says. "I heard Kendra Farnsworth was pretty upset. But I've seen you two together. So I guess you must've patched things up. That's nice."

"Yeah. We're friends."

She gets an expression I can't quite read now. But it's sort of worry mixed with curiosity. Still, she doesn't say anything.

"Anyway, I have a favor to ask. Well, actually more like a job."

So I launch into the whole barbecue thing and how it would be extremely helpful to have someone looking after Nana, and she nods like she really does understand. And I start to feel hopeful.

"I'm sure that *would* be awkward, having *all* the cheerleaders at your house with your grandmother there." Somehow, the way she says this gives me the impression she's making fun of me, and I feel irritated. Yet, it's not like I can say anything. Andrea has the upper hand in this.

"It's just that I don't think I can take care of Nana and host the party too," I say. "You know?"

"Do you think she'd be okay over here? I mean, would it be confusing for her? Would she be disoriented?"

I consider this. Andrea is making a very good point. But I don't want to be bothered with it. I just want this taken care of. I remind myself of how Mom can be when she wants something done and wants it done right. I want to be careful not to sound like that. "I don't know," I begin. "I mean, Nana really likes you, Andrea. You have totally won her over, which I think is really sweet of you. I actually feel bad that I wasn't a better friend to you . . ."

"Really?"

I nod but tell myself to not go too far. To not get carried away. "Anyway, I think if Nana was with you, she'd be perfectly fine. And, don't forget, I do plan to pay you. I already mentioned that, didn't—"

"Oh, that's okay. I don't want you to pay me. I'll just do it—"

"No, I insist. I wouldn't feel right."

"But I like Ruth," she says. It's weird hearing her use Nana's first name. "I'd do it just to spend time with her."

"Why?" I ask suddenly. I mean, I really am curious about this.

Is Andrea really that desperate for companionship? Is she that pathetic?

She sort of shrugs, then looks down at the coffee table. As usual, there's a big black leather Bible there. I think it's her dad's, but every time I was here last summer that Bible was always there. Sometimes it was open. Sometimes not. I asked if her family was religious and at first she said no, but then I discovered they went to church a lot, so I figured she was lying. Probably embarrassed.

"It's kind of a long story," she says. "But the short version is that I like spending time with Ruth because Jesus has put her on my heart. I think she needs me around."

I blink and try not to look too stunned. "What do you mean she *needs* you?"

"Well, she's lonely . . . and she's old . . . and I think she needs me to show her a Jesus kind of love."

"A Jesus kind of love?"

"Yes." Andrea looks up, straight at me now. "Everyone needs to see a Jesus kind of love—that's like love in action."

"Oh."

"So, anyway, I'd be happy to have Ruth over here. But I don't want you to pay me. I feel that would be wrong."

Okay, I'm not particularly fond of this arrangement, but then who am I to argue here? I am desperate. I'll agree to almost anything as long as she'll do this for me. And I am so relieved that she wants to. Really, why should it bug me that she's bringing Jesus into it? It's not like I have feelings one way or the other when it comes to Jesus or God or religion. It's her business, not mine.

"Well, that's great, Andrea. I really appreciate it. I don't even know how to thank you."

She smiles. "Just consider it a gift from God."

"Well, yeah. Okay, I guess."

She sort of laughs. "I know you don't really understand this, Reagan. I don't even expect you to. But I have a feeling that God is at work in both you and your grandma. Now, what day is this barbecue?"

"Next Saturday."

She looks worried now. "*Next* Saturday?"

"Yes, is that a problem?"

"That's the Wild Life retreat weekend."

"What's a wildlife retreat?" Okay, this sounds like something totally weird and I'm starting to wonder what kind of freak she is. Is it even a good idea to leave Nana in her care? Not that I have so many options.

"Wild Life is a youth ministry for middle-school kids. Maybe you've heard of Young Life?"

"They had Campus Life at my old high school," I say, not mentioning that only geeks actually went to the meetings. "Is it like that?"

"I think so. Anyway, Wild Life is like the younger version of Young Life. And this is my first year of being a counselor and I'm just getting to know the kids, and I *have* to go on this retreat."

"You have to?" I feel myself frowning now, getting impatient.

She nods. "I have to go. I'm sorry. Can you have the barbecue some other weekend?"

"No." Okay, now I'm getting mad. I can't believe I came over here and begged and groveled and now Andrea is saying no.

"I really am sorry, Reagan. If I could do this for you, I would."

"But what about all that stuff you said about God and Jesus?" I demand. "You said Jesus wanted you to love Nana—and how she was old and sick and everything—and you're not even willing to do this?" Okay, I know I'm being totally unreasonable and I can't believe how selfish I sound. But I'm desperate.

"Jesus wants me to love the middle-school kids too," she says calmly. "And that was a previous commitment. I can love Ruth during the week and—"

"But I need you on *Saturday.*"

"I can't help you, Reagan."

I stand now. I want to scream at her, but I know that's crazy, not to mention pointless and rude. "Thanks a lot," I say in flat voice.

"So you didn't mean anything you said?" I can hear the hurt in her voice. "It was all just to get what you wanted from me?"

"What?"

"That whole nice act was just so you could use me?"

I don't say anything.

She waves her hand as if to dismiss everything. "It's okay. It's what I should expect. It's just too bad, Reagan."

"What's too bad?"

"That you're becoming like them."

"Them? Who?"

"You know, the mean girls. The ones who will say and do anything to get what they want. For some reason I thought you were different." She shakes her head like she's sorry for me. *Sorry for me!* "But it's okay," she continues. "I suppose you can't help it."

Now, this just really makes me mad, like she thinks she's superior to me. "You don't know the first thing about it," I snap. "Or me. Your life is nothing like mine and I can't expect you to understand how it is to be—to be *popular.*"

She sort of laughs now. "Well, that's where you're wrong, Reagan. But then, you haven't known me that long. The truth is, I used to be one of those girls—a *mean* girl—and I know what it's about . . . the games they play . . . the users walking all over the losers. But then I found a better way. And nothing, not a thing, could entice me to go back to that."

I narrow my eyes and give her a look that's meant to convey I don't believe her. No way could Andrea Lynch ever have been popular. She is a geek. A total and complete geek. Not only is she a geek, but she must be delusional too. Poor thing. If I wasn't so angry I'd feel sorry for her.

"I'll be praying for you," she says as I head for the door.

"Don't bother," I say in a snooty tone.

"Oh, that's okay. I don't mind."

What is wrong with this girl? Is she totally nuts or what? "And don't bother coming to see my grandmother anymore either."

"Why not?"

I turn around and look at her now. "Because I don't think I like the kind of influence you might have on her. I think you're some kind of weird religious fanatic and you're probably trying to convert her to some crazy religion. And I don't think that either my mom or I would appreciate it. So stay away from her."

She blinks and looks hurt. I do not care. I do not freaking care. I walk through her house and past her mom, who looks slightly stunned and I'm sure has been listening. I walk out the door and back to my house, promising myself to never speak to that lunatic again. Some people!

"Where've you been?" Mom asks me once I'm in the house.

"Nowhere."

"Well, do you plan to be home today?"

"Why?"

"Because I'd like to go out."

I remember my plans to hang with Kendra, but I don't mention it. "I don't know why you think someone needs to be here with Nana on the weekends. She's by herself all day on the weekdays, what's the—"

"That's exactly why I think she needs someone here, Reagan. Because she's alone the rest of the week. It seems the least we can do is spend time with her on the weekends."

"I do spend time with her. But do I have to spend every waking minute with her?"

"No, of course not. I just wondered if you'd be around."

"Well, I was going to get some paper plates and things for the barbecue next weekend."

"That shouldn't take long."

"No . . ."

"And you'll be home after that?"

"Yes."

"So, no problem."

"Right. No problem."

She smiles now. "I have to say, Reagan, I'm really proud of how you're helping out around here. The house has been so clean every evening when I get home. Nana seems to be in good spirits. I think you were right about keeping her home with us." Then she opens her purse and hands me some money. "Use this for your barbecue things, sweetie."

I thank her and don't bother to mention that I've had help. No way am I going to tell her how Andrea Lynch has been popping in this week on her little mission of mercy. If Mom wants to think it was all my doing, well, fine. After this, it will be all my doing. Suddenly I wish I hadn't spouted off to Andrea like that. What was I thinking?

I put Nana's lunch in the fridge, turn on the country music channel, lock the doors, and tell her to be good.

She grins. "I'm always good, Reagan."

I nod. "Well, stay out of trouble then." I set the cordless phone by her and remind her which button to push if she needs me. My cell phone number is on speed dial and I've painted the number with red fingernail polish. Even so, I'm not sure she can remember how to do it.

I feel a little guilty as I ride off in Kendra's convertible. But not for long. Soon we are laughing and talking and I am actually having fun. Maybe because Sally and Meredith aren't with us. I put thoughts of stupid Andrea Lynch behind me. I put thoughts about Nana and what she might or might not do today behind me. Today is a day for fun.

And we have fun. Kendra is great at planning a party, and after we get all that stuff, we head over to the mall, where I help her spend a lot of money at Nordstrom. I buy a shirt just to have something to carry around, so I won't look like a loser. Then we go to a new shoe store that carries some exclusive designers, and Kendra buys an awesome pair of red heels by Christian Dior. She plans to wear them for homecoming, since she'll be in the court.

"What are you wearing with them?" I ask.

She shrugs. "I don't know. It's not like it's a big deal. I'll probably just throw something together at the last minute." I act like I get that, but the truth is, I don't. Still, I don't want to look stupid. After that, we stop for a coffee and I notice that it's nearly five. I tell Kendra that I should head for home. She's reluctant, but I insist.

"Want to catch a movie tonight?" she asks as she pulls into my driveway. "Or do you have a big date?"

I laugh. "A big date? Who with?"

"Well, I've seen Jonathan looking at you lately. And he sure seems to like tossing you in the air at practice."

125

"Probably because I'm the lightweight of the bunch. And Jonathan's the smallest of the guys."

"But he's smart."

I nod. "And he's nice."

"He thinks you're nice too."

"Really?"

She nods. "I'm sure of it. And now that I think about it, Jonathan is fairly good friends with Logan. Maybe we could double with them sometime."

"Cool."

"In the meantime, we could catch a chick flick tonight."

"I'll call you."

"Okay."

I feel incredibly happy as I walk toward the house. This feels like life is supposed to feel when you're sixteen and in high school—at least the way I imagine it's supposed to feel. In some ways, my life has never been what I'd call *normal*, although I aspire to it constantly. But today was good. Very good. And I feel relaxed and happy.

These feelings evaporate as soon as I open the door. I see a moccasin in the entry and then Nana, in her pink sweats, sprawled across the hardwood floor, lying flat on her back, eyes closed, not moving.

"Nana!" I scream as I run to her side. "Nana!"

twelve

NANA DOESN'T ANSWER. I FALL DOWN TO MY KNEES AND PUT MY FACE DOWN close to hers, touching her forehead with my fingertips. It's still warm. I put my cheek next to her nose. She's still breathing.

"Nana?" I say more quietly. "Can you hear me?"

She groans softly, then her papery eyelids flutter open. "Reagan?"

"Are you okay?"

"Fell down."

"I see that." I try to remember first aid now. You're supposed to keep them warm. "Stay here," I say, knowing that she's going nowhere. I run and get her blanket and lay it over her. I want to ask her when it happened, how long she's been like this, but I know it's pointless. Time is a concept outside of her grasp these days.

"Did you hurt anything?"

"Yes."

"What?"

She moves her hand down and pats her leg. "Here. Hurts here."

"Okay. Just relax and I'm going to call someone." I walk over to where the cordless phone is still on the table next to her pink chair, pick it up, and call 911. The dispatcher lady takes my information and soothingly talks to me as I wait for the ambulance to arrive. I follow the ambulance to the hospital. It's not until I'm in the ER with Nana that I think to call my mom. I dial her cell phone number and hold my breath as I listen to it ring. She picks up on the third one.

"Reagan?" she says, obviously checking her caller ID.

"Nana fell down," I say simply. "She slipped on the hardwood floor. I think she may have broken something. We're in the ER right now and she's about to get an X ray."

"Oh no."

"She's totally conscious and seems to be in good spirits, considering."

"I'm so glad you were there with her, Reagan."

"I should go, Mom. She's asking a question and no one's in the room right now but me."

"Yes, go and be with her. I'll be there in about thirty minutes, okay?"

"That's fine, Mom."

"That's as soon as I can get there."

"Really, Mom. Everything's under control. Drive safely."

Then we hang up. And I am so relieved that she's not mad at me. Not yet anyway. I don't want to tell her that I was gone when Nana fell. I don't want her to get angry at me for having been out all day. I'm fully aware that this accident might not have happened if I'd been home sooner. Even so, I'm not sure I can admit this to Mom. Besides, what good would it do? It wouldn't change anything.

Nana's getting her X ray done when Mom gets there. "She should be back in a few minutes," I say.

"Was she in much pain?"

"I think it was hurting pretty bad," I admit, trying not to remember her sobs when they loaded her on the gurney. She didn't understand what was going on. I tried to explain that they were helping her, but she thought they were hurting her and wanted them to stop.

"Poor Mother."

"But the doctor gave her something for the pain when she got to the ER. I think she was feeling better before they took her to the X-ray room."

"Did you tell them she has Alzheimer's?"

"I filled out the paperwork when I got here, but I forgot to put it on there. But I did tell the receptionist that Nana has some memory problems and that it's probably Alzheimer's."

"Probably?"

"Okay, most likely."

"Sometimes it's better to just accept the facts, Reagan."

I sigh and look down at my lap.

Mom actually puts an arm around me then. "I'm sorry. I should be thanking you for handling everything so well."

Okay, this is nice, but it makes me feel even more guilty. This might not have happened if I'd stayed home. I'm almost tempted to confess the whole thing. But not yet.

It turns out that Nana has broken her pelvic bone. "It's a painful place to break a bone," the doctor explains, "because it's so integral to all body movements. Whether it's walking, sitting, standing, bending, lying down, using the toilet—you name the activity and the pelvic bone is probably involved."

"Oh, dear." Mom puts her hand over her mouth. "So how do you treat it?"

"In her case, it's just a matter of letting it heal. She'll be bedridden for a while, but then we'll try to get her moving, into physical therapy. If all goes well, she could be on her feet in six weeks."

"Six weeks?"

"In the meantime, she'll be confined to a wheelchair and need a lot of help. What kind of facility is she in now?"

"Actually, she's still living at home with us," says Mom.

"Does she have a full-time caregiver?"

"Just my daughter and me. I looked into an assisted living facility not too long ago. She's on their waiting list."

He frowns. "Assisted living won't take her now."

"Why not?"

"Because she needs too much help. She's at a whole new stage of care now." He writes something on a piece of paper. "Give this place a call. Tell them she'll be released from the hospital in a few days." Then he walks away.

"That seems a little harsh," I say as I watch him heading down the hallway.

"I'm sure he's just being honest with us."

"What's the name of the place?" I ask.

"Martindale Manor," she reads. "I'll give them a call."

I wait in the lobby while Mom calls the nursing home on her cell phone. I still feel extremely guilty, like this is all my fault—on so many levels. And yet what can I do? I consider offering to care for Nana myself, at home. But I know that's not really possible. I have school . . . and a life.

"They can take her," says Mom, looking relieved.

"Should we go check them out first?"

"I don't know if there's any point, since they're the only care facility with an opening right now."

"Is that what they told you?" I feel suspicious now.

"Yes. But they also gave me a couple of other names in case I wanted to shop around."

"Oh."

"We just have to accept this, Reagan. I know it's hard to let her go to this next stage, but maybe it's for the best."

"Maybe." I turn away and head for the restroom. Tears are blurring my eyes now. I just do not see how this can be for the best. And I just do not understand a world where someone as sweet and good and kind as Nana must suffer like this. What is up with that? I wonder how Andrea Lynch would explain a God who does things like this? I have half a mind to call and ask her. But I won't. I will not give her the satisfaction. Besides, she might blame me for Nana's fall. She heard how upset I was when she couldn't watch Nana next Saturday. Maybe she'll think I pushed her.

As I'm standing in front of the sink, my cell phone rings. "Hey, Reagan," says Kendra. "How about that movie?"

So I explain to her about Nana's accident, about finding her on the floor, and, actually crying as I speak, I even confess about the Alzheimer's. Then, to my surprise, Kendra is very understanding and supportive.

"Forget about the movie," she finally says. "I'm just sorry to hear all that you've been through. Poor Reagan."

I sniff. "I'm okay. But it's just been such an ordeal. Sorry to dump on you like that."

"Hey, that's what friends are for." Then she asks which hospital. And I tell her. "How about if I stop by and say hey?"

"Sure," I tell her, although I don't know why she wants to trouble herself. Still, it's sweet. And I think this is just more proof that Andrea was totally wrong about Kendra and my friends. Why did I let that stupid girl get to me?

It's not long before Nana is settled into a room. Mom and I stay with her, just talking and reassuring her that everything's going to be okay. I notice that Mom's not mentioning anything about the nursing home. And maybe that's for the best. It would probably just confuse her anyway.

"When can we go home?" asks Nana for about the sixth time.

"Not today," Mom says again. She glances at me. "I'm going to get some coffee. Want me to bring you something?"

"No thanks."

Shortly after Mom leaves, Kendra shows up with a beautiful bouquet of pink roses and a little pink teddy bear.

"Oh, my!" Nana claps her hands happily and I introduce them.

"Andrea," says Nana. "You look so pretty today."

"No, her name's not Andrea," I say, acting like Nana just got it wrong, although I know she actually thinks this is Andrea Lynch, which makes no sense, except that they're both blonde and about the same height and Nana's got a memory problem. "Her name's Kendra."

Kendra laughs. "Oh, well, Kendra sounds a little like Andrea."

"Yes." Nana nods and smiles. "Kendra, Andrea, Andrea, Kendra. They rhyme. Like LeAnn Rimes. That rhymes too."

I toss Kendra an embarrassed smile and she just laughs and continues to chat nonsense with Nana. It's actually nice having her here and I'm impressed with how easily she goes along with things, how she seems to accept Nana just as she is. Almost like a member of the family. When Mom gets back, I introduce her to Kendra, and I think Mom's actually impressed with my friend.

"Beautiful roses," she says as she moves them closer to Nana's bedside.

"Pretty pink," says Nana happily. I think maybe the pain medication is making her even goofier than usual. But she's so sweet, it's hard not to smile.

"It was so nice of you to come by the hospital," Mom says to Kendra.

"We had planned to go to a movie tonight," I tell Mom. "But I told Kendra that I—"

"Why don't you go?" says Mom. "I can stay here and keep Mother company."

"Oh, but—"

"No, really, Reagan. There's no reason we both have to be here. In fact, maybe we should take turns visiting her while she's in the hospital. It'll help to pass the time for her. You can pop in after school and I'll come during my lunch hour and in the evening. How does that sound?"

"Sounds good," I say.

"So go," she says, waving her hand.

Nana looks a little disappointed to see us leave, but I turn the TV to the country music channel, even though this makes Mom frown, and Nana cheers up. Then I kiss her good-bye and say, "I'll see you later."

"See you at home," she calls. And I just wave.

"She's going to go into a nursing home," I explain to Kendra as we go down in the elevator.

"Does she know that?"

"No. There's probably not much point in telling her. It would either worry her or she'd just forget."

"Getting old must be horrible," says Kendra as we walk through the lobby. "I think I'll ask someone to just shoot me if I ever get so old that I have to be taken care of."

"Me too," I agree. Not that I want anyone to shoot Nana.

I drop my car at my house, and as I get into Kendra's car, I notice that Andrea is outside raking leaves, watching us. She actually waves, but I pretend not to see.

"Do you know that girl?" asks Kendra, who obviously saw her.

"Not really," I say. "I met her last summer when we moved here. She wanted to be friends, but I was like, uh, thanks but no thanks."

Kendra snickers. "Smart thinking. She's such a geek."

This reminds me of something. "I still remember this totally weird thing she told me though." I laugh as if it's really funny. "She said that she *used* to be popular. Like that was going to impress me. I mean, seriously, how pathetic is that?"

Kendra laughs. "Extremely pathetic. But, you know, she actually did used to be slightly popular. Like way back in middle school. Then she turned into this religious freak and no one could stand her anymore. She sort of went from freak to geek."

"And get this," I say, deciding to totally trash her. "She was so desperate to be my friend that she hung out with my grandma." I laugh loudly. "I mean, I love Nana to pieces, but can you imagine hanging out with an old lady just so you could be friends with her granddaughter? Serious Geek Girl."

"That is so lame. Oh, yeah, her name's Andrea, isn't it? That's probably why Nana got my name mixed up with hers."

"Maybe so," I admit. "That's so sweet that you call Nana Nana. She really seemed to like you, Kendra."

"You mean Andrea, Kendra, Kendra, Andrea? Or LeAnn Rimes?"

We both laugh, but I don't think that joke's terribly humorous, since it seems to be at Nana's expense. Still, I have to admit that Nana can be pretty funny.

The movie turns out to be sort of ho-hum, but it's a good distraction from this afternoon's trauma. And by the time Kendra's driving me home, I feel like maybe things will be okay after all. I thank her and get out. I see that the lights are on inside, which tells me that Mom must be home from the hospital. Hopefully Nana will be okay through the night. Maybe they'll give her something to help her sleep.

I go inside through the front door and am immediately hit with the memory of Nana sprawled across the floor. I *so* thought she was dead. I guess I should be really thankful that she wasn't. Still, it was upsetting.

"Reagan?" I hear Mom calling from the kitchen.

She holds up the Nordstrom bag that contains the shirt I got today. "You went to the mall?"

I consider this. "Yeah, just for a little while. After we got the party stuff."

"The receipt in this bag says you purchased this shirt at 3:43."

"Uh-huh." I study Mom. "What are you, like a detective?"

"I'm just curious as to how long Nana was home alone today and whether you were here when she fell."

"Well, no, I wasn't here when she fell, Mom. I never said I was."

"You gave me that impression, Reagan."

"Sorry. It was all pretty upsetting."

"So do you have any idea what time it was when Nana fell? Or how long she might've been on the floor like that?"

I shake my head no.

"Well, her lunch is still in the fridge."

"Oh."

"So it's possible she was on the floor for several hours, Reagan."

Okay, this is really starting to bug me. "Is that my fault, Mom?"

"You gave me the impression that you were going to be home for most of the day."

"So?"

"So did you lie to me?"

"No!"

"But you were gone for several hours?"

"I didn't really watch the clock, Mom. And I was having fun, so it's possible that the time got away from me." I stare back at my mother and wonder why she can be so mean sometimes. "What are you saying? Are you trying to blame this on me, Mom? Is Nana supposed to be my responsibility? Am I supposed to take care of her around the clock?" Okay, I know I'm stepping over the line and asking for it, but Mom has pushed my button. "Sometimes I actually wonder if that's the reason you adopted me, Mom. Just so you could have a little Chinese slave girl to wait on you. And then you could have her wait on your mother too. Was that your plan?"

Mom's eyes grow wide. "I can't believe you'd say something like that, Reagan! When I think of all I've done — "

"What about *me*, Mom? What about all I've done for you? And I'm the kid here. I didn't ask to be brought into this home. I didn't have any choice."

"Reagan Margaret Mercer!"

"Sorry, but that's how I feel sometimes!"

For the first time that I can ever remember, my mother is speechless. She just stands there with her jaw hanging down, staring at me as if I'm a perfect stranger. And maybe I am. Sometimes I think I don't even know myself anymore.

"Well." She shakes her head. "I think we've both had a long day. We're very stressed and have probably said some things we don't mean."

I just nod and walk away. Okay, I got off pretty easy just now. Still, I think that might've been the closest thing to an apology I've ever gotten from that woman. Honestly, when it comes to meanness, sometimes I think my mother might've written the book on it!

thirteen

JOCELYN AND CHAD ARE ACTUALLY DATING NOW. THIS HAS PUT JOCELYN IN a very jolly mood, which should make varsity squad a lot more pleasant, but it seems that Sally is in a perfect snit.

"What's eating Sally?" I ask Kendra as we go to the cafeteria together on Wednesday. "Is she like having really bad PMS?"

"More like fits of jealousy."

"But I thought she really didn't like Chad. Is she actually jealous of Jocelyn?"

"She's not jealous of Jocelyn, Reagan. She's jealous of you."

"Me?" I blink as I pick up a tray. "Why? I'm not even dating anyone, although Jonathan has sure been getting friendly. I'm guessing you said something to him?"

"Just a little something. By the way, how's the plan with Logan going? You said you were going to talk to him again today."

"And I did." I grin. "And we talked mostly about you."

"Really?"

"Yeah. I think he really does like you, Kendra. But he doesn't like to be pursued by a girl."

Kendra nods like the light just went on. "Of course! That explains everything, Reagan. You're such a genius!"

I laugh as I pick up a green salad and a packet of dressing.

"So tell me, why is Sally jealous of me? If that's even true, which I doubt."

"It should be obvious, Reagan. She thinks you're replacing her and she doesn't like it."

"Oh."

"But don't worry about it. I assured her that I have room in my life for lots of friends."

"That's good." I just hope Sally bought this, because I really don't want that girl for an enemy. Kendra is one thing, but Sally is something altogether different. Sally seems ruthless in a way. Like she would resort to almost anything. The whole bit with the uniform switch still sends chills down my spine when I think about it. I did offer to loan Jocelyn the money to pay for the alterations if she promised not to tell anyone that I did. I have a strong suspicion that both Sally and Kendra would *not* appreciate this little intervention. To be honest, the only reason I did this was to salve my conscience a bit. It seems I am piling up more and more things to feel guilty about—and it's not fun.

"How's Nana?" asks Kendra as we find seats.

"She moves to the nursing home today," I tell her.

"You think she'll be okay?"

"The staff there assured my mom that she'll be fine," I say, although I'm not convinced. "We packed up a bunch of her things last night and Mom is taking them over today. I'll go visit her after practice."

"You need any moral support?"

"Thanks," I say, unsure as to whether I want Kendra to see Nana in this new setting, which might not be too great. "I think I'll be fine. And Nana will probably be a little disoriented. It might be better if I go alone."

She nods and smiles sympathetically. "You're a good girl, Reagan."

I laugh. "Yeah, right!"

***

The nursing home is a nightmare. Okay, that's my opinion. But, really, it's so much worse than the first place we visited, I wouldn't even know where to begin to describe it. But for starters, it really stinks. The whole place smells like a big filthy toilet. Totally gross. And the residents there are all either about to die or just plain crazy. Consequently they're either heavily sedated or screaming. Really, it's like a house of horror.

Poor Nana. She looks so frightened as she lies motionless in her bed. Her eyes are wide and I can tell she feels as if she's been locked in some kind of terrible prison.

"Am I going home now?" she asks hopefully when she realizes it's me. She pushes the covers away as if she's going to get out of bed.

"No," I say in a soothing voice, putting the pale blue bedspread back on. "Your pelvic bone is still broken. You need to get better, Nana."

"I can get better at home," she persists.

"No," I say again. "You need to be here where people can help you."

"No one helps me here."

"Really?"

"I'm all alone. I haven't had anything to eat. And no water."

"Really?" Now, this is alarming. "Let me go see what I can do." So I go out to the nurse's station and demand to know what's going on.

"They all say things like that," the overweight woman tells me.

"That they haven't eaten?"

"Yes. They eat and then forget."

"Really? You can assure me she's had food?"

"Check her chart, if you like."

So I look at her chart, but then I think they can write whatever they like on those charts. Who would know?

"Can I give her something to eat now?"

"Dinner is on its way."

"Oh."

So I decide to stay long enough to make sure she eats. As nauseating as it is to smell food amid all those other smells, I decide I can do this for Nana's sake. The tray comes and it's some kind of noodle-and-beef mess that's the color of pavement. Nana turns her nose up at it. "I don't want that."

"Come on," I urge. "Just try it?"

So she takes a bite. Then another. Before long she's eaten most of it.

"How about the applesauce?"

"That's not applesauce."

"Yes, it is," I say. "Try it."

She takes a bite, then thinks about it. "It's not applesauce." Still, she eats all of it and I begin to feel a tiny bit better.

"Mom will be here soon," I say, glancing at the clock. "I'm going to go now because I have homework to—"

"I want to go," she says in a childlike voice. "Home?"

I reach out and take her hand. "Nana, this is home for right now. Okay?"

She makes a face. "This is not home."

I lean down and kiss her. "I love you, Nana," I say. "I wish I could take you home."

She looks hopeful.

"I'll tell you what," I say. "If you get all well, I will take you home."

She smiles. "I'll get all well."

"Good." I squeeze her hand. "Mom will be here in a few minutes."

She's still holding on to my hand and I actually have to pry my fingers free. I wave. "Bye-bye, Nana."

She looks like she's about to cry, but she holds up her hand and curls her fingers, mouthing *bye-bye*. I feel like my heart's torn in two as I walk out of her room. Really, it's my fault that she's here. First of all, I talked Mom out of letting her stay in the assisted-care place, which now seems like the Hotel Ritz compared to this sleazy place. Second, I wasn't there when I promised to be and that's when Nana fell and broke her pelvis. So it seems quite obvious. It's my fault that Nana is in this horrible place. Somehow I need to think of a way to get her out.

I'll think about that *after* the barbecue.

Mom and I have been like the old proverbial ships in the night this week, which I think is a good thing after that fight we had. I think we both needed some space. But when Mom gets home tonight, she comes and knocks on the door of my room. I hope I'm not in trouble.

"Yeah?" I say and she opens it.

"Nana said you didn't come to see her today."

"Yes, I did, Mom."

"Why would she say that?"

"Because she can't remember."

"But she remembered before, when she was at the hospital."

"That's probably because she's traumatized over being in that horrible nursing home." Then I go into a detailed description.

"Okay, it sounds like you were there," Mom concedes.

"That place is nasty," I continue. "I wouldn't put a dog there. I can't stand that Nana's there. Can't we find something better?"

"I've already called around."

"When?" I challenge.

Mom gives me a look, but then answers. "Today. After seeing the place last night, I wasn't too pleased." She shakes her head. "I'm even less pleased today. Nana said she hadn't eaten all day."

I sigh. "Yeah, she said the same thing to me. So I stayed while she ate dinner." Then I describe exactly what Nana ate.

"The Alzheimer's is getting worse."

"I know." Again, I feel guilty. Why did I fight Mom on that first place?

"I arranged to have her chair taken over there tomorrow. I thought it might comfort her to see it. And the physical therapist said she might even be able to get up and sit in it."

"How about putting a TV in her room?" I suggest. "She loves the country music channel."

Mom nods. "I hadn't even considered that. Okay, I'll make sure that happens too."

Then it gets very quiet. Neither of us says anything. I realize that for the first time in years, it's going to be just Mom and me now. I'm not sure how I feel about this. Already I miss Nana's laughter and antics. I miss her fun spirit and goofy sense of humor. Mom and I tell each other good night, and she goes out and quietly closes my door.

Then I turn off my computer and to my surprise I begin to cry. I'm not even completely sure why. I just feel so lonely. So lost. Is it simply because Nana is gone? Or is it something more? I wish we could go back to how it used to be. I wish I was a little girl again, coming home from school to find Nana in the kitchen stirring up Rice Krispie treats and adding M&M's to the mix and then letting me eat the sticky goop right out of the bowl. Why is growing up so hard to do?

fourteen

"Can you give me a ride to the cleaners?" Jocelyn asks me on Friday after school. "I thought I'd get Chad to take me over, but it turned out he had a dentist appointment at three."

"Sorry, I need to go visit my grandma right now." I sling the strap of my bag over my shoulder. I've been trying to be civilized to Jocelyn lately, but I'm also trying to keep my distance. Kendra has made it perfectly clear that she doesn't want anything to do with Jocelyn. Which means if I want to remain Kendra's friend, maybe even her best friend, I need to keep Jocelyn at arm's length or even farther. To be honest, that's fine with me. Ever since Jocelyn and Chad became a couple, Jocelyn's been more loud and obnoxious than ever. She even got into a slight argument with Falon over how to properly do a stag jump. Give me a break!

Jocelyn's face takes on a pout as she jerks on her jeans. "But I have to get there before five, Reagan."

I feel Kendra's eyes on me now and I know she's listening. "And why *exactly* is that my problem?" I turn and stare at Jocelyn like she's not worth my time.

Jocelyn glares back at me. "Because *you're* a cheerleader and *I'm* a cheerleader and if I don't get to the cleaners, I won't have a uniform to wear to homecoming tonight—and that will make us all look bad."

The girl makes a point. "And why is your uniform at the cleaners? I didn't think you'd even worn it yet."

"Because that's where they're doing the alterations. My mom dropped it off for me on Monday."

"Pity your mom didn't pick it up for you too."

"She has to work late tonight."

"Whatever." I glance at my watch, wishing I could end this conversation and be on my way. "Okay, where is this particular cleaners anyway?"

"Over on the east side, on Lombard."

"Well, that is near my grandma's nursing home."

Kendra is next to me now, smiling. "Oh, Reagan, why don't you be a sport and pick up the kid's uniform for her."

I try not to blink in surprise. "Well, I guess I could give you a ride over there, Jocelyn, since I'm going that way. But you'll have to sit and wait while I visit with my grandma," I warn her. "Because I don't have time to drive you all the way back home and then go clear across town again."

"Why don't you just pick up the uniform for her?" suggests Kendra.

I shrug, trying to figure out why Kendra's being so nice to Jocelyn. "Sure, I guess I could do that."

Jocelyn looks truly relieved as she fishes a wrinkled claim ticket from her wallet and hands it to me. "Thanks!" But then she gives me this funny look, like she wants to say something but can't. And that's when I remember that I had offered to loan her the money for the alterations, but I made her promise to keep this to herself. I think that's what's on her mind. And my guess is she's broke right now and can't afford to pick up her uniform anyway. Really, maybe Jocelyn should just drop out of cheerleading if she can't manage her life any better than this!

"So is this all I need?" I ask her, hoping she'll get my drift and play along. "Is it all paid for and everything?"

"Yeah," she says lightly. "You have to pay for alterations up front." She narrows her eyes at Kendra now. "It was pretty expensive too, but not nearly as bad as buying a whole new uniform."

Kendra makes a *tsk-tsk* sound. "Such a pity that happened, Jocelyn. Next time I'm sure you'll be more careful when you order something online."

"Thanks for the helpful advice." Jocelyn turns around and continues dressing. I can tell she's furious, but I also know she's trying to control herself since she realizes I am doing her a big favor.

"Want to walk to the parking lot together?" asks Kendra.

"Sure," I say in a cheerful voice. Nothing like the tone I was using with Jocelyn.

Once we're out of the locker room, Kendra begins to talk in a low voice. "I have just come up with the most delectable idea for a prank that we can play on Jocelyn tonight." Then she giggles and tells me her devious plan for me to loosen up one of the seams on Jocelyn's uniform so that she'll be in serious need of more safety pins tonight.

"I can't do that," I tell her.

"Why not?" She looks seriously disappointed in me.

"Well, for one thing, I'm not even sure how to do it. I mean, I don't know the first thing about sewing or unsewing or whatever it is you're suggesting. Besides that, I'll be visiting Nana for about an hour or so. Then when I get home I'll barely have enough time to get ready for the game, drop off Jocelyn's outfit at her house, and make it—"

"No, no, you don't drop off the outfit at her house. You call her and tell her you're running late, just like you said you would be, and you tell her you'll meet her at the school with it. In the stadium restroom. And you'll have to get there right before the game starts. I'll make sure Sally and Meredith are in there too, as a distraction you know."

"Even so," I say reluctantly, "I wouldn't even know how to do that to her uniform."

"No problem," says Kendra suddenly. "You give me the alterations ticket and I'll pick it up at the cleaners for you and do it myself. I'll drop it by your house before the game, and then you can deliver the goods. Just make sure you call Jocelyn and tell her about running late and how you'll need to meet her in the restroom in the stadium, since the girls' locker room will be full of the other team's players by then. You can do that, can't you?" We're standing by her car now, and her voice is getting a little impatient. Then she smiles. "Trust me, Reagan, this is going to be such a hoot. It's something we'll still be laughing about at our twentieth reunion."

I'm still not too sure about this. "What exactly are you going to do to her uniform anyway?" I ask.

She shrugs. "Nothing that can't be fixed. I promise. And if anything goes wrong with her uniform"—she holds up her right hand now, like she's making a pledge—"I swear I will make it right and I will *give* Jocelyn *my* uniform."

I consider her promise. I think I can trust her on this. And it would actually be kind of nice if Kendra did give Jocelyn her uniform, since I have serious doubts whether the altered elephant-sized uniform will even look right. "Okay," I say, slapping her still raised hand in a high five. "It's a deal."

She throws her arms around me in a hug. "This is going to be so fun!"

"See you at my house before the game then?"

"I'll be there around six thirty. Okay?"

"Perfect."

This is my third visit to Nana in the nursing home, but it is just as sad and depressing as the first time. Even so, I try to put on my happy face. I try to pretend like this is such a great place, and aren't the nurses nice, and I'll bet dinner is going to be delicious. Yeah, right.

Nana is not buying it. She is quieter than usual, just sitting there in her bed and staring toward the window. It's like her spirit is broken, and seeing her like this makes me hurt deep inside.

"Nana," I say, taking her wrinkled old hand in mine, "if you can just get better, maybe you can come home."

She shakes her head. "No. Diane said no. I can't go home."

"Mom said *that*?"

She nods now, tears filling her eyes.

"Well, I don't think that's right," I say. "I'll talk to Mom, Nana. I think if your pelvic bone heals up, you can come home. Even if we have to get someone to come take care of you, you need to come home, Nana."

This cheers her up a little, but I know I'm making a promise I may be powerless to keep. Still, I can't imagine how Mom can be so coldhearted. Okay, maybe I can imagine it. But it's wrong. It's all wrong. And I plan to discuss it with her. And if it turns into a big fight, well, so be it. Of course, I won't discuss it with her until after the barbecue tomorrow. No sense in messing that up.

When Nana's dinner comes, I tell her that I have to go. I explain about the football game and she actually seems to understand, like she remembers what football is, although it sounds like she thinks I'm a football player. I try to explain but then wonder why. Instead I kiss her and tell her to get well soon.

"Have fun playing ball," she says as I head for the door.

I wave and tell her I will.

When I'm out in the lobby, I first call Kendra to check on the status of her prank.

"It's going to be perfect," she assures me. "I've got it all ready, and it's still in the package and you cannot even tell it's been tampered with. I am good!"

"Or bad."

She laughs. "I'll drop it by like I promised. Have you called Jocelyn yet to tell her to meet you at school?"

"That's what I'm about to do."

"This is going to be so fun."

I hang up, then call Jocelyn's number. "Hey, I'm running late," I tell her. "I'm still at the nursing home"—which is true—"and my grandmother's had a hard time with her meals lately. I need to stick around while she eats dinner." Okay, not so true.

"What about my uniform?"

"Don't worry," I say. "I've got it. Let's just plan to meet at the stadium. You can change in the restroom there, can't you?"

She complains about this, but I tell her it's the best I can do. "Do you want me to just leave my poor grandmother right now?"

"Well, no."

"Good, because she is having a hard time of it, Jocelyn. This place is a nightmare and I don't think the nurses even do their jobs."

"Oh. Sorry."

"See you later," I say as I walk to my car. "I need to go help my grandmother with her dinner now." That old "liar, liar, pants on fire" rhyme runs through my head as I drive toward home. And although I try to rationalize this, my conscience is really starting to bug me. Still, what can I do? It's like this thing is already in motion, and Kendra would get mad at me if I backed out at the last minute. I remind myself how Kendra promised to replace Jocelyn's outfit if anything goes wrong. That's worth a lot. Even Jocelyn would be happy with that little arrangement.

I've never been much of a prankster, and for Kendra's sake, I just hope I don't blow it tonight. I push thoughts of the prank to the back of my mind as I get dressed for the game. Glad that Mom's not home yet, I crank up my CD player and lose myself in the music. Fortunately it's not loud enough to block out the doorbell.

"Here are the goods," Kendra announces when I answer the door. She hands me what looks like a perfectly normal cheerleading outfit, neatly hung on a wire hanger and encapsulated in clingy dry-cleaners plastic.

I don't know what to say. My mouth feels dry, and everything in me is shouting, *Don't do this!*

"By the way," says Kendra, "that Jocelyn is a little liar. She hadn't paid a cent for the alterations. The woman told me they never charge until you pick it up and approve it. I had to pay for it myself."

I just shake my head and feign surprise. "Man, Jocelyn must've thought she was going to stick me with the bill. Really nice."

"Well, I didn't really mind paying for it." Kendra laughs now. "Just as long as I get my money's worth."

"I'm sure you will." I suddenly notice that she's really dressed up. "Wow, you look great, Kendra." That's when I remember she's part of the homecoming court. *Try to keep up, Reagan.* Kendra has sort of played down this event and claimed they don't get too dressed up. Nothing like my old school—I was homecoming princess for the sophomore class last year and had to wear a formal.

"Thanks." She holds out a foot, showing off a gorgeous high-heeled Christian Dior that I happen to know was expensive.

153

"You think this outfit looks okay with these?"

"You look absolutely fantastic and those shoes are killer! I'm sure you'll be crowned queen tonight."

"Oh, you're too sweet," she calls happily. "See ya at the game!"

I do a little more primping, waiting until the very last minute before I go out to my car. I've barely pulled onto the street when my cell phone starts ringing. I check my caller ID to see that it's Jocelyn. It figures.

"I'm on my way right now," I say in a rushed voice. "I barely had time to change my clothes."

"Well, I'm waiting in the restroom," she says impatiently. "Hurry!"

I can hear the pep band warming up as I park my car and head toward the stadium. My arms are loaded with my duffle bag, purse, and Jocelyn's uniform, and my heart is pounding as I walk into the bathroom. My plan is to appear hectic and slightly frantic.

"It's about time," says Jocelyn.

"Yeah," snips Sally, who is checking her makeup in the mirror. "We thought we were going to have to raid the girls' locker room with the away-team football players still in there to get Kendra's uniform."

I breathlessly shove the outfit toward Jocelyn. "Sorry, but I have a lot on my plate. It took extra time to go to the cleaners for you, and I have that barbecue tomorrow, and on top of this my grandmother's not doing very well . . ." My voice breaks slightly, adding a touch of realism.

"Poor Reagan," says Meredith as she helps Jocelyn into her outfit.

"Watch out for my ponytail," warns Jocelyn. "I don't have time to redo it."

"Wow, I can't believe that's the same outfit," says Sally with an approving smile. "It really fits you now."

"It's a little tight," says Jocelyn, tugging at the top.

"No, it's perfect," Meredith assures her.

Jocelyn sort of hops up to see herself in the waist-high mirror. "Really? It's not too tight?"

"It's no tighter than mine," says Sally.

"You look great," I tell her. And that's the truth. I'm actually wondering if Kendra really did anything. Maybe this prank is really on me. And that would be fine. Maybe Kendra was testing me, curious to see if I'd go along with something that crazy. Whatever the case, I can't see that there's any problem. That is, until Jocelyn turns around to stuff her other clothes into her duffle bag. That's when I notice that her top has a seam down the middle of the back—not a very neat one—and it's a seam that our tops don't have. The skirt has the same sort of thing. I swallow hard, step back, and bite my tongue. This has got to be Kendra's workmanship.

"Well, I'm going out there now," announces Sally. "You guys ready?"

We all follow her out there, and once we're on the field, I can tell that several of the girls are in on the joke and trying not to laugh. I mostly just try to keep my distance from Jocelyn. I don't want to blow it. We do our regular warm-up chants as the stadium fills up. The goal is to get the crowd pumped up and excited. And then, as our football team enters the field, bursting through the butcher-paper banner stretched between the goalposts, the pep band begins the fight song and we begin our dance routine. As usual, Jocelyn and I are in the center of this routine because we're the shortest. And when we finish up the routine, Jocelyn will be at the top of the pyramid. I consider the irony of this and how she fought me for this position at practice today.

"Reagan is always on top," she complained to Falon. "She and I are about the same size, so why can't I be on top for a change?" Falon reluctantly agreed, I think just to shut her up.

The band is still playing enthusiastically as we quickly get into the pyramid formation and Jocelyn climbs on top. Her shoes dig into my shoulders as she stands up straight, and I'm thinking she probably weighs ten pounds more than me. I see her spread her arms in a wide V, teetering just slightly. We hold the pyramid for the usual few seconds and then I feel Jocelyn going into the jump dismount now, performing a flip as she goes down and is caught by one of the guys. And the crowd cheers.

I'm concentrating on my own stunt now, a smaller flip that lands me soundly on my feet. And, just as I'm about to go into a handspring, I hear hoots of laughter from the stands and I see Chad staring to my right with a totally stunned expression. I turn to see what's up, and that's when I notice Jocelyn is standing still with both hands clasped over the front of her chest, covering her bra, which isn't even a sports bra. Ben is standing a few feet away, holding her blue and white top and looking slightly amused.

"Give it to me!" Then she screams a word at him, one that will get her into trouble as far as the cheerleading contract goes. He tosses her the top, which is split down the back, but when she reaches out to catch it, bending down and leaning forward, her skirt, which was already hanging low, bites the dust. And now she is standing in front of the stadium in her underwear, not even pretty underwear. The crowd roars like they think this is the pregame show.

In that split second, Jocelyn tosses me a glance that I think could maybe kill. Then she gives me and everyone else the old middle-finger salute, grabs the pieces of her uniform, and like a flash (or a flasher?) tears out of there, running past the entire football team lined up and ready for the announcer to begin. But they just laugh and wave at her as if they're enjoying the entertainment too.

Falon is the only cheerleader who isn't laughing. She's not even smiling. She looks shocked and angry and I can tell we're in trouble. The announcer makes a comment about cheerleading outfits not being as sturdy as they used to be, eliciting another good laugh from the audience, and then he starts announcing the players.

With only seven girls now, Falon makes an adjustment in our lineup for the yells and routines. Being tallest, she takes the center, putting the shorter girls on the ends. No one argues with her. It would be pointless. It feels like it's going to be a long night.

Fortunately, things seem to get back to normal by halftime. Oh, people are still talking about the "stripper" cheerleader. And Jocelyn never does come back. Falon says, "That's fine, because if she did come back, I'd send her home anyway. She broke her contract." This makes me feel bad, since it's not really her fault. I mean, sure, she should've watched her mouth. But I feel guilty about helping to sabotage her. I know that was wrong. And it takes a lot of the fun out of the game for me.

I'm a little surprised when Kendra is crowned homecoming queen. Oh, I knew she had a good chance, but I actually thought Falon was going to win. I overhear someone saying that Kendra got the sympathy vote because she didn't make cheerleader this year. I'm wondering what kind of vote she would've gotten if everyone knew she was behind what happened to Jocelyn tonight. Or maybe they wouldn't care. They did seem pretty entertained by the whole thing.

I can't admit this to anyone, but I don't really care when our team loses the game. In some ways, I think we deserve it. But I pretend to be bummed, just like everyone else. I just want to go home and forget this night.

"You are coming to the dance, aren't you?" asks Kendra as we're gathering our stuff.

"Oh, sure," I tell her, although I'd rather not go.

"Good." She gets close to my ear now. "Because I just told Jonathan that I wanted to hang with you and him and Logan tonight, and he seemed to like that idea. He's going to talk to Logan."

"Cool," I tell her, forcing a bright smile. But as I take my gear out to my car, I'm thinking I should feel a whole lot happier than this right now. I mean, here I am, barely one month at my new school, and I made varsity cheerleader, I have a cute and popular guy who really seems to like me, and my almost-best friend is homecoming queen, rich, and beautiful. Really, isn't that about as good as it gets?

Instead, I feel totally miserable. What is wrong with me?

fifteen

DESPITE FEELING TORN AND GUILTY, AND UNABLE TO GET RID OF THAT IMAGE of Jocelyn's face tonight, I put on a good show when I get to the dance. I'm sure no one could possibly suspect that I'm feeling so bummed. After a while, my mood begins to change. I lighten up and before long, I'm actually having fun. Jonathan is a good dancer and I can tell he likes me, and I think I want to get to know him better. Kendra is sort of playing hard to get with Logan, which seems to be working for her. She takes turns dancing with several guys, including Jonathan, but during the last few dances, Logan moves solidly in and takes control. By the end of the evening, Kendra seems happy.

As I drive home, I wonder if she feels any guilt for what happened to Jocelyn tonight. I also wonder how it will all pan out. Knowing Jocelyn, she probably won't take this lying down. I'm not sure if it's that red hair or something else, but I know the girl is a scrapper. And I'm guessing tomorrow's barbecue will be interesting.

***

As usual, Mom is working even though it's Saturday. She actually offered to stay home and help with the barbecue, but I assured her that I'd be fine and that Kendra would be here before too long. Kendra offered to handle all the food today. At first I said, "No, that's too much." But she insisted. "That's what friends are for," she assured me last weekend. And then I agreed.

"I hope to get back to a normal work schedule in a month or so," Mom told me as she left this morning. I nodded, although I seriously doubt this. Among other things, I'm pretty sure my mom is a workaholic. I remember hearing Nana say that word once, back when I was too little to understand the meaning. But now I get it. And I think it's true.

"Everything looks very nice," says Kendra as she helps me to get things ready for our guests. "Your mom has good taste in interior design."

"Thanks," I tell her, but I know she's just being nice. I've seen her house and it's like something out of *Architectural Digest*, a magazine I've only seen at the doctor's office.

"Do you think Jocelyn will come today?" She slides a big bowl of some really scrumptious-looking potato salad into the fridge. Her caterer made it, as well as a bunch of other things.

"I have no idea," I say as I set one of her boxes on the counter. "But I know she's a fighter and I sort of think she'll make an appearance."

Kendra laughs. "That was so funny last night. I think I'll be laughing about it for weeks to come."

"Too bad she had on such ugly underwear," I say, then wish I hadn't.

Kendra laughs even louder. "Well, at least they weren't granny panties. That would've been really bad." She pulls out an apron that says Kiss the Cook and ties it on. Then she takes out a goofy-looking chef's hat and puts it on. "If you don't mind, I'll take care of the barbecuing."

"Really?" I can't believe my luck. "You'd do that?"

"I would for you, sweetie." Now she frowns. "Unless you think the others will mind me being here. I am, after all, just an alternate."

"I don't think anyone will mind. Well, except maybe Falon, but she's outnumbered."

"Jocelyn might mind."

I shrug. "I have a feeling Jocelyn will have her sights set on me today."

"Then you'll need me here for moral support."

So it's settled. Kendra is staying. And I can't believe how much better this makes me feel. Especially when Jocelyn arrives thirty minutes early. She stands at my front door with her ruined cheerleader uniform in her hand and the angriest expression I have ever seen on her face. Seriously, if the girl was armed, I'd think this was about to turn into a Lifetime movie.

"Why did you do this?" she asks in a voice that is seething with anger.

"I didn't *do* that," I say, opening the door wider so she can come in. Of course, this could be a mistake. Maybe I should slam the door shut and lock it. But between Kendra and me, we should be able to keep this girl in line.

"Oh, hi, Jocelyn," calls Kendra from the kitchen. "Want a soda? I've got these really great organic—"

"No, I do not want a soda," snaps Jocelyn. She glares at Kendra. "Man, you don't even wait until the body's cold, do you?"

"What?" Kendra gives her an innocent look.

"Oh, don't tell me you didn't hear the news."

"What news?"

"Falon called me this morning to tell me that I'm on probation."

Kendra shrugs. "Well, that's not much of a surprise, is it? I mean, you obviously broke the contract last night, in front of like hundreds of people too."

Jocelyn holds out the uniform, shaking it in front of us. Then she turns to me. "I *know* you did this, Reagan."

I hold up my hands in a helpless gesture. "Did *what*?"

"You messed with my uniform."

I just shake my head and look her straight in the eyes. "I swear to you, Jocelyn, I did not mess with your uniform. All I did was deliver it to you. I thought I was doing you a favor."

"Yeah," says Kendra. "That's not very nice to accuse Reagan of something like that, Jocelyn. Your alterations person obviously needs to go back to sewing school." She sort of laughs. "Although how she ever shrunk that giant uniform down to a small size seemed nothing short of miraculous. Well, until it fell apart."

"You expect me to believe the alterations person did this?" She shakes the uniform under Kendra's nose.

Kendra steps back, stands up straighter. "What other explanation could there be?"

Jocelyn points to me. "She did it. And I know why she did it." She points at Kendra now. "For you. Admit it. You're both in on this."

I actually put my hand on Jocelyn's shoulder now, a little trick I've picked up from Kendra. "Look, Jocelyn, I swear to you that I did nothing to your uniform. I was at Nana's nursing home all afternoon. Sheesh, you could even go over there and ask if you don't believe me. Don't ask Nana, since her memory's pretty bad. But you could ask at the front desk. You could look at the book. I signed in."

Jocelyn narrows her eyes and looks directly at me. "You swear you didn't do this?"

I hold up my hand. "I swear!"

Jocelyn cusses now.

"Hey, girlfriend," warns Kendra, "you're going to have to clean up that potty mouth if you want to keep being a cheerleader."

"Forget it!" she yells. "I'm finished. It's not worth it." She's on the verge of tears now. "I can't afford another uniform, and this one will never work." She looks at Kendra, then at me. "I'm sick of cheerleading."

"I'm sorry," I say, hoping to sound as sincere as I actually feel, because I really am sorry.

She looks at me with watery eyes. "You really didn't do this?"

"No, I didn't."

She nods sadly. "I didn't really think you could be that mean." Then she turns like she's going to leave.

"Aren't you staying for the barbecue?"

She sort of laughs. "Are you kidding?"

"Come on," urges Kendra. "Stay. We have a ton of food. Just stay. You'll feel better if you do."

She turns and faces us. Tears are streaming down her cheeks now. "Falon told me that probation means I don't do *anything* with the cheerleaders for two whole weeks. No practices, no games, no uniform, no barbecue, nothing. Not that it matters, since I really do plan to quit. I'm so done with this."

I go over to her now and actually hug her. "I'm sorry, Jocelyn."

She wipes her nose on the sleeve of her sweatshirt. "Yeah, whatever."

Then she leaves and the kitchen gets very quiet. If this is a victory it sure doesn't feel like it. I wonder if Kendra feels as guilty as I do.

"Wow," she finally says. "I honestly didn't think Jocelyn would give up *that* easily."

I shake my head. "Me neither."

"Do you think that was for real?"

I just shrug.

"Or is this just a setup?" Kendra gets a troubled brow.

I sigh loudly. "I don't know. But I'm sure tired of it—I'm tired of all this crud—all this meanness. It takes the fun out of everything."

"Why don't you put some music on," suggests Kendra. "It might lighten things up. And you better start getting the table outside ready. Put the paper plates and napkins out. And, oh yeah, I've got a bouquet of flowers in the back of my car you can get. I'll take care of things in here."

I look at Kendra, standing over the sink wearing the apron and funny hat, and it's hard to really envision her as the mean girl. She looks more like a pretty clown at the moment. And yet . . .

"I do feel bad for Jocelyn," she says in a quiet tone, as if she's been reading my thoughts.

"You do?"

She nods. "But maybe it's for the best."

"Yeah. Maybe." Then I go out and set the table.

The cheerleaders start arriving and my spirits begin to lift. I try to push thoughts of Jocelyn out of my head, but it's not easy since she's pretty much the hot topic of the day. They can't quit talking about her performance last night. I don't mention to anyone that she was just here.

"And what are *you* doing here?" Falon questions Kendra when she finds her out on the patio, turning hamburgers and hotdogs on the gas grill. Everyone gets pretty quiet now, waiting for Kendra to answer.

But Kendra just makes a small bow. "Last night's queen is today's galley slave. I am here only to serve." Several people snicker.

"Yeah, right," says Falon, as if she's not convinced.

"Hey, I couldn't have done it without her," I say. Then I glance at Kendra. "And did you guys hear the latest news?" I ask. Suddenly I have everyone's attention. "Should I tell them?" I ask Kendra.

She shrugs. "It's up to you."

"Jocelyn stopped by a little while ago . . ."

"And?" demands Meredith hopefully.

"She's quitting cheerleading," I say.

Everyone but Falon, Chad, and me erupts into a cheer.

"That's too bad," Chad says after they settle down.

"Maybe it's for the best," says Falon. She studies the group now, like she's trying to make up her mind about something. "I know that Jocelyn wasn't totally to blame for what happened last night, but she's been kind of a loose cannon and not exactly the sort of image that we like to present as varsity-squad cheerleaders."

"That's right," says Meredith. "We need to clean up our image."

Falon glares at her. "We all need to work at it."

"I think that Jocelyn was a big part of the problem," says Sally. "Whenever there was a fight or disagreement, she always seemed to be in the middle of it." Then Sally goes on to remind us of a few times when Jocelyn mouthed off, and pretty soon everyone seems to agree.

"So should I tell Coach Anderson that we have a consensus about this?" asks Falon. "We're okay with Jocelyn quitting the squad? We don't think there needs to be an investigation or anything?"

Everyone except Chad and me chimes in their agreement. And I don't think anyone really notices that we're not saying much.

"Well, good," says Falon. "That's a relief. Because I have good news for you guys." She smiles broadly. "We've been invited to the state competition."

Now everyone starts cheering and jumping around.

"And you know they cut down on invitations this year. I really didn't think we'd make the list." Falon looks at Kendra. "I guess it's a good thing you got that uniform and stuck around for practices. That's going to help a lot."

Kendra smiles. But not smugly.

"Not that this is totally official," warns Falon. "I still have to speak to Coach Anderson."

Even so, it feels official. And everyone seems happily relieved. And I have to admit that the general spirit of the cheerleaders is way better than usual. It seems like everyone is getting along better than ever, and I have to wonder if what they're saying is true. Maybe it is because Jocelyn is no longer with us. Even so, I still feel bad. And guilty.

But it's funny how you can get used to suppressing bad feelings if you have to, and I think I am becoming a pro. It helps having Jonathan around. I'm starting to see that he really is into me. And that's fun. I haven't had a boyfriend since Aaron Bradshaw during the last part of my freshman year. I think I'm ready for this kind of attention. I suppose I'm sort of eating it up too. Anyway, I'm feeling a lot better about life and cheerleading and everything after we're done eating. The barbecue seems to be a success. Everyone seems to be having a good time, just hanging out in the backyard, practicing stunts, and talking.

Eventually I go to the kitchen where Kendra is starting to clean up.

"You don't have to do that," I tell her.

"I know," she says. "But why not?"

Then I give her a big hug and actually kiss her on the cheek. She laughs. "What's that for?"

"Your apron." I point to the front. "It says Kiss the Cook."

"What is this?" asks Sally in a sharp, suspicious tone. "You guys turning gay on us?"

"Yeah, right!" I throw a dishtowel at her.

"Well, it looked pretty weird."

"Hey, lots of girls kiss," says Kendra lightly. "Some even kiss on the lips. Reagan only kissed me on the cheek."

"Reagan kissed Kendra?" says Ben as a couple of them join us in the kitchen. "Man, what have we been missing?"

"It was a kiss of gratitude," I tell him, suddenly feeling embarrassed. "She's been a huge help to me with this barbecue." Then I point to the apron. "Besides, that's what it says on her apron."

So the boys take their turns kissing the cook too. Kendra seems to enjoy this, but I still feel weird about the way Sally tried to turn that on me. It's like she has her claws out and is ready to tear into me—a lion on the prowl. Kendra mentioned that Sally was jealous. But you'd think she'd be thankful to me for backstabbing Jocelyn and helping Kendra get onto varsity.

We get things somewhat cleaned up—I'll have to really attack it later before Mom gets home—then we go back outside and practice some stunts. And just as Jonathan is doing a toss with me, I notice Sally sauntering out through the French doors with something white in her hands. And as Chad catches me, I realize it's a pair of Nana's Depends. I thought for certain that all of Nana's stuff was out of here by now. We boxed everything up and the mover guys took some things to storage and others to her nursing home, including her case of Depends. But suddenly I remember that bottom drawer in the downstairs bathroom.

"What are *these*, Reagan?" Sally asks as she dangles the disposable pair of underpants in front of everyone.

I feel my cheeks getting hot as I walk over to her. I'm trying to think of a clever response, but nothing comes to mind. So I decide to tell her the truth, that they belong to my grandma.

"Got a little bed wetting problem, do we?" She waves the Depends around like a flag, then laughs.

"Those belong to Nana—I mean *my grandmother*." I reach over and snatch them from her and wad them up.

"Yeah, right." She rolls her eyes with a wicked smile. "Hey, it's no big deal. We all have our little secrets, don't we, guys? So what if Reagan is a bed wetter with a fondness for chicks and—"

"Shut up, Sally," says Jonathan, and I want to hug him.

"Oh, feeling defensive, are we?" She laughs. "I'm just joking with you guys. And, really, does it matter if Reagan wets the bed?"

"My grandmother used to live here," I try to explain, feeling totally humiliated. "She has Alzheimer's and needed to wear Depends."

"Sure, Reagan," says Sally. "Whatever you say."

"I've *met* her grandma," says Kendra in an angry voice. "And that's the truth. So lighten up, Sally. You're just jealous that I'm friends with Reagan now. You need to grow up."

Sally glares at Kendra. "Hey, don't go postal on me. I just thought it was funny that Reagan wears diapers. Sheesh, we all got a good laugh at poor Jocelyn last night running around in her underwear. It seems only fair that we share the jokes around."

"Well, your joke is not funny," snaps Jonathan.

"And why are you snooping around my house anyway?" I ask her.

She shrugs. "I didn't know you had things to hide." She laughs again. "I guess we all have things to hide, don't we, kiddies?"

Kendra gets close to Sally now. Just a few inches from her face.

"And I happen to know you have a few things to hide too, Sally. You sure you really want to play this game? You could get hurt!"

Well, that shuts Sally right up. But it puts a damper on the party as well. Falon, disgusted with our general immaturity, says she has a date with Caleb and has to go. Soon everyone trickles away until it's just Kendra and me.

"I can finish cleaning up," I tell her. "Really, I totally appreciate all your help today. I could not have done it without you."

She smiles. "Like I said, that's what friends are for."

sixteen

"Come on," says Sally. "Let bygones be bygones, Reagan. I really want you to come to my party. I want you both to come."

It's been nearly two weeks since homecoming. Jocelyn has officially quit cheerleading. Kendra has replaced her. And things have been going relatively smoothly. Until today. Today, Sally is trying to talk me into coming to her birthday party.

I glance over at Kendra and she just shrugs. "I'm not going if you're not going," she says as she zips her jeans.

Naturally, this only seems to irritate Sally more. The truth is, I would love to totally boycott Sally's birthday party—and for that matter Sally too. She apologized to me over the stupid Depends incident, but I've kept a safe distance from her since then. I do not trust that girl. She's extremely jealous that I've replaced her as Kendra's best friend. I have no doubts that she would take me out if she got the chance. And I don't plan to give her the chance. Furthermore, I can't believe she really wants to have a slumber party. I mean, seriously, didn't that go out with middle school? I even pointed that out to Sally a few days ago. I could tell it hurt her feelings and made her mad, but I didn't really care.

"Come on, you guys," she urges us. "It's my eighteenth birthday—my last high school birthday party. I want it to be like the good old days. And it's going to be girls only. We can totally let our hair down." She looks at Kendra hopefully. "Remember my fourteenth birthday party when we snuck out and TP'd Coach Hanley's house?"

Kendra sort of laughs, then nods.

"Come on," says Sally again. "I want all the cheerleaders to be there. I've even invited Jocelyn. That should show you that I'm trying to be a nice girl."

"Is Jocelyn actually coming?" I ask, surprised by this since Jocelyn has been keeping a pretty low profile.

Sally shrugs. "I don't know. Probably not."

"How about Falon?" asks Kendra, glancing over to where Falon is just emerging from the showers.

Sally rolls her eyes. "I doubt it. I think she and Caleb plan to elope this weekend."

We laugh at this. Then we make fun of the lame outfit Falon wore to school today. Not so she can hear us, of course; we're not that stupid. If we want to dis some girl who's within hearing distance, we make sure that it's never Falon.

"Come on, you guys, it'll be fun," says Sally. "You can't hate me forever, Reagan. I know I've done some lame things, but didn't your other friends do stuff like that? Didn't you guys ever play tricks on each other back at your old school?"

"I guess."

"You have to forgive and forget."

Kendra looks at me. "So, whadya think?"

I shrug. "I don't know."

"It is her birthday," says Kendra. "Maybe we should give the girl a break. We can always ditch the party if things don't work out."

"I guess," I say reluctantly.

"Okay, we're in," says Kendra.

"Such enthusiasm," says Sally, acting hurt.

"Sorry," I tell her. "Maybe we can muster more by Saturday."

"Yeah, that'd be nice."

***

I've decided that I don't like myself anymore. It's not a good feeling, but it's the truth and I feel like I need to be truthful about at least one thing. The rest of my life feels mean and hypocritical and dishonest, and I don't know what to do about it. Besides backstabbing Jocelyn, which still haunts me, I have also hurt a person I dearly love. Nana. Oh, I haven't done anything to her directly. But I have quit visiting her. I have abandoned and betrayed her. At first I skipped a day. Then I skipped two. Now it's been a full week since I've been to see her. Mom keeps nagging me and I keep making excuses. I'm afraid I'll never go back there again. I'll never see Nana again. It's like I can't. And, consequently, I feel like a stake has been driven into my chest. Into the place where my heart used to be. Now it's just this hard, cold, painful spot that slowly grows bigger. I think someday I will be made entirely of steel.

It's Saturday morning and Mom is at work. I am home alone trying to think of a way to bail out of Sally's stupid slumber party. Give me a break. How ignorant does she think I am? Of course, I realize that if I don't go and Kendra does go—well, that could be stupid too. It's better to be around to defend yourself than to be missing in action and discover the following week that you got totally trashed by your so-called friends. Still, I don't know what to do.

I hear the doorbell ring, and although I'm still in my flannel pajama bottoms and a tank top, I go to see who it is. At least it won't be Jonathan. I know this for a fact since I broke up with him after the game last night.

"Why are you so bummed tonight?" he asked me for like the fiftieth time.

"I don't know," I told him again. "Why don't you quit asking me?" Of course, that somehow evolved into an argument. He assumed I was bummed because I wanted to break up. I assumed he was simply using that as an excuse because he wanted to break up. One thing led to another and the next thing I knew we had broken up.

The funny thing is that today I don't really care. I don't think I care about much of anything as I go to see who's at the door. But when I look through the peephole and see that it's Andrea Lynch, I'm tempted to pretend I'm not home. And yet I'm curious as to what she wants. So I open the door.

"Hello?" I say with a frown.

"Hi, Reagan." She sticks her hands into the pocket of her hoodie and I take this as a hint that it's cold out there. "Do you have time to talk?"

I shrug, opening the door wider. "You want to come in?"

"Thanks."

Then we're sitting in the family room and I am wondering what gives this girl enough nerve to just come over here uninvited, to sit here on our leather couch and act like she's perfectly at home.

"I want to talk to you about Ruth."

It takes me a couple of seconds to realize that she means Nana. "What about my grandmother?" I ask suspiciously.

"She misses you."

"How would you possibly know that?"

"Because I've been visiting her."

"What?" I begin to envision her as a stalker. Perhaps she's using

Nana to get to me. This is so pathetic and weird.

"Our youth group has been going to Martindale Manor for the past couple of years now."

"Why?"

"It's just something we do, a way to reach out to people. We visit the patients there, take them little gifts, spend time with them, no big deal."

"Why do you do that?"

She shrugs. "Because that's what Jesus would do."

"Oh, right." I try not to roll my eyes now.

"I know you don't get that, Reagan, but that's just because you're not a believer yet."

"Yet?" I stare at this pushy girl and wonder what makes her so confident and self-assured. She certainly doesn't have the appearance of someone who would normally gain my respect. And yet, to be honest, I do sort of respect her. And this bugs me.

"Anyway, I was surprised to see that Ruth was there. She actually remembered me. Well, not my name, but she remembered me. And so I've been going to see her when I can. She asked me about you . . . and sometimes she even calls me Reagan."

"She calls *you* Reagan?" Now this makes me want to scream and shout and throw this stupid girl out of my house.

"It's only because she misses you," she says calmly, "and because she's confused."

"Still."

"Why did you stop visiting her?"

I put a chenille-covered pillow on my lap, then pull it up to my chest. I think I want to conceal the fact that there is a stake driven in there.

"I mean, I know it's hard," she continues. "Martindale Manor isn't exactly the nicest nursing home in the world."

"You're telling me!" I sock the pillow now. "I think they send people there to die."

"Which is one of the main reasons our youth group decided to commit to it."

"Because you think the people there are going to die?" I demand hotly. "Do you go over there and try to save souls, just so you can put some sort of a notch on your belt?"

Andrea sort of laughs. "Not exactly. Oh, we do share the gospel with them sometimes. But mostly we just want to love them the way Jesus does—you know, unconditionally. And they respond to that kind of love. It's amazing, really."

"I'm sure it is."

"Well, I can see you're not really interested in all that," she says. "Mostly I wanted to let you know that Ruth misses you."

"Right."

She leans forward slightly now, just sort of peering at me. "You seem really unhappy, Reagan."

I shrug, look away.

"I know it's none of my business, but if you ever want to talk . . . well, you know where I live." Then she stands.

"Wait," I say suddenly. "I'm just curious about something."

She sits back down. "What?"

"What made you become . . . you know, like you are now?"

"You mean how did I become a Christian?"

"Yeah, I guess."

"You really want to know?"

I consider this. "I think so."

So she tells me about how she used to be sort of like me. She was fairly popular and she was striving to remain popular, but she was unhappy. She pauses now and looks at me. "Have any of your friends ever told you about Lisa?"

"Lisa?"

"Lisa Carlyle."

"No. Who is Lisa Carlyle?"

"More like who *was* Lisa Carlyle." Andrea sighs. "Lisa was my best friend. She was also good friends with Kendra, Sally, and Meredith."

"So what happened with Lisa?"

"She died."

I stare at Andrea, trying to determine if this is a true story or something she's concocting just to reel me in. Maybe she thinks I'm like one of her old folks at the nursing home, like she can get me down on my knees and use me for another notch on her belt. "I take it I'm supposed to ask how she died."

"Have you ever heard of the choking game?"

"*Choking* game?" I make a face. "That doesn't sound like a very fun game to me."

"No, I didn't think so either. Kendra was the one who taught us how to play it."

"Kendra?" Now, I find this hard to believe, but I decide to go along with her.

"Yes. She had this slumber party in eighth grade and she showed us how to do it there. Even then, Kendra was the most popular girl. If you wanted to be liked, you listened to Kendra. If Kendra said, 'Jump,' you said, 'How high?'"

I give her a look that's meant to convey my skepticism, but I don't say anything. I wish she'd just finish her story.

"Anyway, we all tried it—the choking game. Everyone except Lisa. She was scared."

"Okay, back up the truck," I say. "What exactly is the choking game?"

So she explains how you use a rope or belt or something to constrict the blood flow around your neck. "You keep it there long enough to make you dizzy and sometimes you pass out. Kendra claimed that you could have visions or something. I guess some people find it euphoric, and I've heard it can actually become addictive."

I suddenly remember a friend who used to do something like that. She called it zonking, but she didn't tie anything around her neck. Even so, I thought it was bizarre. And it's pretty hard to believe that Kendra could be into something like that. In fact, that's just what I tell Andrea. "I'm sorry, but I find this hard to believe. Kendra is not that stupid and I cannot imagine her playing a game like that."

"Well, we were only fourteen at the time. I'm sure she's not into it anymore. But back then I have to admit it was sort of fun and exciting. Besides, like I said, if Kendra encouraged you to do something, you usually did it. If you didn't, you were ostracized."

"So Lisa was ostracized?"

"At first, but Kendra kept pushing her. She actually sort of bullied Lisa into trying it. Kendra didn't want anyone to leave her party without trying it. I think she was afraid they'd tell someone and she'd get into trouble, but if we all did it, we'd be in it together. You know, sort of like a drinking party."

"I guess."

"Anyway, when Lisa finally tried it, she actually enjoyed it. She did it several times at the party. And I guess she kept doing it on her own too. I suppose it's possible that she became addicted to it. I remember telling her that I thought it was stupid and she shouldn't do it anymore. And she told me she had quit. But apparently that wasn't the case. And one day she was doing it by herself in her room. She must've passed out for a long time, long enough that she never regained consciousness."

I frown. "She *died* from playing the choking game?"

Andrea nods and her eyes get wet. "She died of asphyxiation."

Okay, I feel bad for Andrea, but I'm having a hard time buying this. It seems impossible to think someone could actually die from playing this silly game. I wonder if she's just messing with my head. Or maybe she's trying to turn me against Kendra. "So are you saying it was Kendra's fault that this girl—Lisa—died?"

"No, not exactly, but Kendra did pressure her into it. I mean the first time. I suppose it was Lisa's choice to continue doing it. Still, it made me totally rethink the direction of my life."

"And that's how you became religious?"

"It made me start searching for answers."

"And you think you found them?"

"When I discovered that God has a plan for me, and that I can have a personal relationship with Jesus, and that Jesus has forgiven me and given me a new life, yes, I knew I'd found the answers."

"Well, good for you."

"So you're not looking for any answers?"

I press my lips together and wish this obnoxious girl would just go away.

"I'm not trying to push you, Reagan. It's just that you do seem unhappy. And, whether you can admit it or not, I'm pretty sure you are searching. Or you're about to start searching."

"I'm just fine," I tell her, standing up now. "But thanks for the sermon."

She stands too. Then she smiles. "Sorry. I hadn't really meant to preach at you. I only wanted to let you know that your grandmother

179

misses you."

"So I've heard."

Then I lead her to the door and tell her to have a nice day, and it's all I can do not to slam it behind her. What a bunch of hogwash about how it's Kendra's fault that some girl died in middle school. Like that's supposed to be my problem now? *Puh-leez.*

For whatever reason, I decide that I will go to Sally's party after all. I even go out and buy her a birthday card and present—a pair of silver hoop earrings that I think are pretty cool. The more I think about it, the more I believe Andrea Lynch is crazy—and that whole story about the choking game is probably bogus. Maybe she's jealous that I'm friends with Kendra instead of her. Whatever it is, I decide not to think about it.

seventeen

SALLY'S HOUSE ISN'T TOO FAR FROM WHERE I LIVE. ALTHOUGH IT'S AN OLDER neighborhood, it's not a crummy one like where Jocelyn lives. And her house is actually kind of cool, a turn-of-the-century Victorian, although it's in need of a few repairs. I've ridden over with Kendra, and instead of knocking she opens Sally's door and walks right in.

"Hey, you two," says Sally happily. "You finally made it. Everyone else is already here."

"I like your house," I tell her as I hand her the gift and card. "It must be a fun place on Halloween."

She laughs. "Oh, yeah, we used to decorate big-time when my sister and I were kids. We loved making this fake graveyard and everything. But Betsy's in college now and I don't really bother with it anymore. I think the trick-or-treaters actually get more scared when it's not decorated. Especially if there aren't many lights on."

"Yeah," says Kendra. "It can look pretty spooky."

It turns out that Sally's parents are gone for the weekend. I think this is a little odd, but then, Sally is turning eighteen. Maybe they assume she's all grown up now. And she seems to think so too, since she's got a variety of alcoholic beverages on hand. I try not to look surprised.

"Good thing Falon's not here," I point out as I pretend to sip the drink she's mixed for me. It's not exactly a Cosmo, like Kendra made, but it's kind of sweet and pinkish. Still, I think it tastes awful and I don't plan to finish it. However, the rest of the girls seem to be enjoying their drinks. I wish I'd known this was what tonight's party was going to be like. I'm not sure I would've come. Even now, I'm wishing I'd driven myself. I could just slip out, and I doubt that anyone would even notice.

Sally points her finger at me. "You don't seem to be having much fun, Reagan. Don't you like your drink?" Then her eyes light up. "Oh, yeah, I almost forgot what's in the fridge."

"What?" asks Meredith.

"Jell-O shots."

Everyone acts like this is the greatest idea. And soon the girls are popping them like they're candy.

"Come on, Reagan," urges Sally. "Try one!"

"I'm fine with my drink," I say.

"You've hardly touched it," she shoots back at me. "You're really not much of a party girl, are you?" She turns to Meredith. "Reagan is our little teetotaler."

"Want some tea?" asks Meredith. They both laugh like that's the funniest thing. I'm sure the alcohol makes it seem so.

"I don't want to be a wet blanket," I say quietly to Kendra as she pops another Jell-O shot into her mouth, "but do you realize how much alcohol is in one of those things?"

She just laughs and shoves a red one toward my mouth. "Come on, Reagan. Lighten up. Have some fun."

I take the shot with my fingers and even pretend to taste it, but when no one's looking I toss it into the garbage disposal.

"I'm gonna do eighteen of these," Sally announces. "For my birthday. Anyone wanna join me?"

"Eighteen is a lot," says Meredith.

"My sister did twenty-one last month for her twenty-first birthday," brags Sally. "And she was just fine." She laughs. "Well, I think she had a pretty good hangover."

Kendra is counting out eighteen shots now, arranging them in colorful circles on a plate. "This can be your birthday cake," she says, holding up her rainbowlike arrangement. "But let me get some candles first. And then we'll sing."

Okay, I've had enough. I follow Kendra into the kitchen and as she searches the cupboards and drawers for candles, I tell her I'm not feeling well and that I think I'll go.

"Really?" She turns and looks at me as if she doesn't believe me.

I make a face like I'm in pain. "Yeah. It's cramps and I've got them really bad."

"Take some Midol."

"I did. I took a lot," I lie. "And they're worse than ever."

"Oh." She frowns. "You want me to drive you home?"

I shake my head. "No, I think I'll just walk. Sometimes that helps with cramps. Sorry about this. Tell Sally I'm sorry."

"Hope you feel better."

So I slip out the door. But it's dark outside and I'm not sure I want to walk. I'm not far from home, but having grown up in Boston, I've been taught that a girl doesn't walk by herself after dark. I sit down on Sally's porch and try to think. What should I do? If I call Mom, she'll want to know what's up. I can tell her I don't feel well and that might work. But she might have questions too. I think about the fact that Sally plans to do all those Jell-O shots for her birthday. And she's already acting slightly drunk. What if she gets sick? What if Kendra gets sick? I've heard stories of alcohol poisoning, but I've never actually been around anyone that sick. Jocelyn was pretty bad the night Kendra had her party, but I doubt she downed as much as Sally plans to.

I remember the story Andrea told me about her friend Lisa who died from playing the choking game—a game she was initially pressured to play. I think about the pressure my friends have put on me tonight, pushing me to drink and do Jell-O shots with them. Is that really how friends treat each other? Or maybe they're not really my friends. Maybe they're just using me—the same way I'm using them, if I dare to be really honest. Do any of us actually care about each other? I think of how mean we can be, how selfish, how cruel. Is that what friendship is supposed to be?

I feel extremely lonely. And I really want to talk to someone. If Kendra wasn't in there getting drunk, I'd try to talk to her. But I know how that would go. She would skim over the surface, pretend that she was listening and that she cared, and then she would say something light and move on to something like shoes or boys. I wonder if that's how they handled it after Lisa died. Did they just move on, pretending like it never happened? Did they forget about her and simply return to thinking only of themselves, devising new ways to put others down and make sure they came out on top? We always think we have to be on top.

I remember the night Jocelyn insisted on being on top, I mean literally. And now she's escaped this girl-eat-girl world. I almost envy her. At least she's not still caught in the middle of the fray anymore. She doesn't have to remain on the lookout constantly, making sure no one stabs her in the back. I already took care of that for her. I really do hate myself.

Despite the darkness, I leave the porch and start walking toward my house. It's only about nine, but with no moon it feels much later.

I feel tears slipping down my cheeks now, quickly chilling in the autumn air. I no longer care that I'm walking by myself at night. I almost hope that I'll be mugged. At least that would put an end to how miserable I'm feeling right now.

I'm finally in my subdivision, several blocks from my house, when I hear a car pulling up behind me. I don't even look at it, but just keep walking, quickening my pace a little and wondering if I should run. The car drives very slowly, moving at the exact same speed as I am walking, staying right next to me. My heart begins to pound and I feel certain that thugs are going to jump from the vehicle and knock me over the head, drag me into their car, and—

"Reagan?" says a girl's voice.

I turn and look. "Andrea?"

She smiles. "Need a lift?"

"Uh, yeah, sure." I hop into her car, which is this old Volkswagen Carmengia that her dad's been helping her restore. It's actually a pretty cool car. "Where are you going?" I ask, trying to act natural, like I'm not seriously traumatized.

"Just coming home from youth group. I decided to leave early tonight. How about you?" She puts the car in gear.

"I was at a party. I decided to go home early too."

She turns and kind of peers at me now. "Are you okay, Reagan?"

I'm not sure if it's the kindness in her voice or the relief that I'm not actually being mugged, but the floodgates open and I start to really cry. She just drives slowly without saying anything. I appreciate that. Then we're in front of my house, but I don't open the door to get out.

"Want to go get a coffee or something?" she offers.

"Uh-huh." I choke out the answer, then put my face in my

hands and sob as she drives away from my house. I am a mess. But somehow I manage to stop crying by the time she parks in front of Starbucks. I'm sure my eyes are red and probably swollen. Still, I don't even care. For the first time in a long time, my image seems unimportant. We go inside and order our coffees, then sit down, and I tell her everything. Absolutely everything. I even confess to her the prank we pulled on Jocelyn. I finally end my tale with Sally's drinking party tonight, admitting that the reason I left was because I felt pressured to drink with them. I just totally dump on the poor girl. And she just listens. When I'm done I ask her if she's shocked.

She just shrugs. "It's not all that surprising to me. But it doesn't sound like much fun either. I know I couldn't live like that, at least not and live with myself as well."

"I don't think I can either," I admit.

"But I also know that if it wasn't for Jesus in my life, I'd probably be doing those very same things." She shakes her head. "In fact, I'd probably be with Sally right now, drinking and doing Jell-O shots—probably competing to see if I could do more than anyone else."

I blink. "Really?"

She nods. "Seriously, if God hadn't intervened in my life, well, I don't know where I'd be right now. Maybe I'd be dead like Lisa."

I frown and take a sip of my now lukewarm vanilla latte.

"So what are you going to do about it, Reagan?"

I look up at her. "What do you mean?"

"I mean what are you going to do? Are you going to keep living like that, going down that dead-end road? Do you like being miserable?"

"No, of course not." I sit up straighter, feeling slightly defensive.

"Sometimes you have to make a decision."

"What if I don't *want* to make a decision?"

"*Not* making a decision is the same as making one. It's like saying you *like* how things are going, that you want to keep heading in the same direction. But I think that's a bad choice. I mean, why would you want to live a life that makes you miserable? It makes no sense."

I nod. I think I understand what she's saying. Maybe I even agree with her on some levels. Just the same, I'm *not* ready to fall down on my knees and embrace her religion. I hope that's not what she's attempting here.

"Okay . . ." I say slowly. "I guess I don't want my life to keep going like this. I do hate the lies. I hate the meanness. And I really hate *being* mean. Most of all, I hate being such a hypocrite and . . . I hate myself."

"Then change."

"How?"

She smiles. "See, that's the catch. I don't know if it's really possible to change all by yourself. I mean, you can act differently. But *real* change — the kind that starts on the inside and transforms you — only comes when you give your life to God."

I consider this. And maybe it makes a tiny bit of sense, but I'm not really buying into the whole thing. Plus, I don't think I'm ready for a big step like that. I don't want to turn into someone else. I just want to be happy. For some reason this makes me think about my friends. Okay, they're not perfect, but then neither am I. Suddenly I feel seriously worried about them.

"Look," I say to Andrea. "I can't really wrap my head around all of that right now. And the truth is, I feel seriously worried about Kendra and the rest of the girls. It's like they're really out of control."

"Do you think someone could get hurt?"

I tell her about Sally's plans to do eighteen Jell-O shots for her birthday. "And she was already drinking before that. I mean, I couldn't believe how much alcohol was there. And there were only seven of us. Six now."

"What do you think you should do?"

"I don't know, but the more I think about it the more worried I get."

Her forehead creases and I can tell she's really pondering this.

"Any ideas?" I ask hopefully.

"Well, I was just wondering what Jesus would do — that helps me make decisions sometimes."

I try not to roll my eyes. "So what do you think Jesus would do?" I'm sure she's about to tell me that I should call the police or their parents or do something responsible like that.

She smiles. "Well, he'd probably go back and join them."

"You mean he'd drink with them?"

"Well, no. I mean, he drank wine sometimes. But he wouldn't drink if it was against the law, like if he was underage. And he wouldn't drink to get drunk. But I do think he'd stay with them and try to make sure that everyone was okay."

"Right."

"Although I'm not suggesting you should —"

"That's it," I say, getting to my feet. "I'll go back there and just hang with them. That's no biggie."

"I don't know . . ."

"No, that's a great idea. I'll just quietly slip in and make sure they're okay. My overnight bag is still there and it won't kill me to spend the night."

She nods. "Yeah, you're probably right." And like a real friend,

Andrea drives me back to Sally's. "I'll be praying for you," she says, "and for them too."

I thank her and slip back inside. The music is cranked up and I can hear voices and laughter. The girls are in the living room. Meredith and Kendra are dancing and the others are sitting on the chairs and couch, teasing each other and saying things that make no sense. Sally's not talking at all. She's leaning back on the couch with her eyes half shut in a weird sort of way.

"Hey, look who's back," yells Kendra in a slightly slurred voice. "Feelin' better now, are ya, Reagan?"

"Yeah," I say, perching on the arm of the couch. "I'm okay now."

"Ya wanna dance?" asks Meredith, holding her hands in the air as she staggers around and finally collapses on an easy chair, which she only partially connects with before she slides down to the floor in a heap of giggles. The others laugh.

I glance over to where the partially full bottles of alcohol are still scattered about on the bar, along with a mess of dirty glasses, plates, used napkins, and some platters of party food. I decide it can't hurt to clean up. So, trying to appear unobtrusive, I quietly begin putting some of the dirty dishes, as well as the bottles of liquor, away. I throw the remaining sloshy Jell-O shots down the sink. I put the dishes in the dishwasher, and I hide the liquor under the sink. Then I freshen up the food platters and walk around the room encouraging the girls to have something to eat. I carry a plate with sandwich wraps that are cut into neat little wheels. "Want some?" I ask, acting like I'm a waiter at a cocktail party.

"No thanks," groans Meredith, putting a hand over her mouth as she looks away from the food. "I've had enough." She does not look well.

"Do you need to get to the bathroom?" I set down the platter and take her by the arm. I think she's about to hurl and I do not want to have to clean that up. I rush her down a hallway and luckily find the bathroom in time for her to throw up. Unfortunately I don't get her all the way to the toilet, but she does manage to hit the big claw-foot bathtub.

"Thanks," she mutters as she sits in a heap on the bath mat in front of the tub.

"Are you going to be okay?"

She nods. "I think so. I'll stay here though." Then she curls up on the bath mat like she plans to take a little nap.

I decide to go check on the others.

"Who put the booze away?" asks a girl named Haley as she leans on the bar.

Ignoring her question, I turn to Kendra, who is munching on chips. "Did Sally really do eighteen shots?" I ask.

She laughs and glances over to where Sally is now completely conked out on the couch. "She mos' certainly did."

"Is she going to be okay?"

"She jus' needs to shleep it off."

"But that was a lot of alcohol."

She nods dramatically. "Yeah, impressive." She glances over to the bar. "Hey, where's the rest of the Jell-O shots?"

I just shrug.

"I need ten more to cash up," she says. "I tol' Sally I could do eighteen too."

"Keep eating your chips," I tell her. Then I go to check on Sally. Her face is really pale and when I call her name, she doesn't respond. "Sally," I say again, this time gently patting her on the cheeks, which feel cool and clammy. Still no response. I check her pulse and can barely feel it. I give her a little shake. Still no response. In fact, it seems she is barely breathing.

"Kendra," I call out. "I think Sally needs help."

Kendra comes over, leans down, and looks at Sally. "Nah, she jus' needs to shleep it off, Reagan. Lighten up, will ya?" Then she goes over and turns up the music and starts dancing again. I want to yell at her and tell her she's wrong, but what's the point? I really believe Sally is in danger and I know what I need to do. I go into the kitchen, locate a phone, and call 911. It's weird because until this month, I'd never called 911 in my life, and now this is the second time. I hope it's the last. I try to calm my voice as I tell the dispatcher what I think is wrong, carefully describing the symptoms. Maybe he will tell me it's no big deal and not to worry.

"How much did your friend have to drink?" he asks after he's assured me that help is on the way.

"I don't know exactly," I tell him. "She had several drinks and then she did eighteen Jell-O shots."

"Are you with your friend now?"

"No." I tell him this isn't a cordless phone and I can barely reach out of the kitchen with it. Why didn't I use my cell phone?

"You'll have to put the phone down. Then you'll need to go and turn your friend on her side so that if she vomits, she won't choke. Then cover her with a blanket. Paramedics will be there in about three minutes. Don't hang up the phone until they arrive."

"Okay." So I set the phone down and go over and do what he said. The weird thing is that the party, such as it is, just continues. It's like they don't even notice what I'm doing or recognize that there might be a crisis going on here. The music is still loud. Kendra and the others are still laughing and dancing, occasionally tripping over each other and tumbling onto pieces of furniture. It seems

everyone is completely oblivious to the fact that Sally is unconscious and barely breathing. All her so-called friends are too wasted
to notice or care.

It's not until the paramedics are actually inside the house—just
as I'm turning down the blaring music that drowned out their
sirens—that the girls become partially aware of what is going on.
Then, as two of the paramedics begin to work on Sally, I tell the
third one about Meredith. "I just checked on her," I say, "and she
seemed to be asleep, but—" That's when the police arrive. I don't
know why I hadn't even thought about that. But now I know we're
all going to be in trouble. And the truth is, I really don't care.

eighteen

"I THOUGHT YOU WERE MY FRIEND," KENDRA HISSES AT ME AS WE RIDE IN THE backseat of the patrol car to the police station. It looks like being arrested has sobered her up some.

"Yeah, I thought so too," I say in a tired voice.

Five of us are on our way to the police station, where I've been told we'll be charged for underage drinking and our parents will be called. Sally and Meredith are on the way to the ER, where they will be treated for alcohol poisoning. Meredith was conscious but unable to stand and walk on her own—sick enough that they decided to take her in. On the other hand, Sally looked bad. They put an oxygen mask on her and loaded her onto a stretcher and she never even moved. Her face was so pale I felt certain she might be dead. Even now, I'm not sure she wasn't. Kendra still insists that Sally was perfectly fine, just sleeping it off, and that I overreacted and got everyone into trouble for no good reason.

"Well, just for the record, you are no longer my friend," snaps Kendra.

"Yeah, whatever."

"As far as I'm concerned, *you are dead*, Reagan Mercer."

At first I don't respond. But then I remember something. "Like Lisa Carlyle?"

Kendra turns and stares at me. "What do you mean?"

"I mean the girl you taught the choking game to—the one you pushed and pressured until she finally played. Isn't she dead to you too?"

Kendra narrows her eyes, glaring at me as if she'd like to kill me. I return her stare until she finally looks away. Once we're at the station, we are all questioned separately. Now, I realize I'm not on the witness stand, but in my statement I tell the truth, the whole truth, and nothing but the truth. I am so sick of lies and games. And even though I know the truth will get me into trouble too since I did have a couple of sips of alcohol, it is such a relief to be honest.

"Well, that takes care of it then," says the officer who questioned me.

"Now what?" I ask, fully expecting to be locked up or taken to a juvenile detention center or something equally grim.

"Now you go home," he says as he finishes writing something. "Just like the rest of your friends. You are released to the custody of your parents, and you'll be notified when you need to appear in court."

"That's it?"

He sort of smiles. "Well, hopefully that's it, Reagan. I get the impression that you're not the kind of girl I'll see in this situation again. Right?"

I nod. "Definitely."

He holds up his notes. "The judge will take your help and cooperation into consideration. I'm guessing the charges will be dismissed."

I feel somewhat optimistic.

"Your mother is probably in the lobby waiting."

Of course, as I walk toward the lobby, the hope completely

vanishes. I wonder if I wouldn't rather be locked up in jail than face my mother. I am so not looking forward to this. Not at all. But to my surprise, my mom seems slightly happy to see me. She actually hugs me and simply says, "Let's go." At first, I assume this is because she doesn't want to make a scene in public, but even after we get in the car, she doesn't yell or fume or anything. Finally, I can't take it.

"Mom," I say, "go ahead and scream at me if you want. I can handle it."

"Oh, Reagan," she says. "Is that how you think I am?"

"Well, you do have a temper," I remind her. "And you always get mad when I blow it. You always expect me to be, well, sort of perfect."

Now she doesn't say anything and I figure I've probably hurt her feelings. Neither one of us speaks until we get home. And, although it's nearly one in the morning, she finally says something.

"The policeman told us what happened," she begins. "He came out and spoke to all the parents at once. He didn't have all the facts, but he said a drinking party got out of hand. He said one girl wasn't intoxicated and had the clarity of mind to know that a couple of her friends were in trouble. He said her calling the paramedics was a very brave thing to do. And then he told us who the girl was. And, although I was fit to be tied when I got the first phone call, I was proud of you when I heard the whole story."

I blink back surprise. "Proud?"

"I know it sounds silly, I mean considering all the other things I could choose to be proud about — making good grades, being a cheerleader, helping with Nana, staying out of trouble — well, for the most part anyway."

I sigh and feel like I'm about a hundred years old.

"I know it wasn't easy moving here, Reagan. Then this thing

with Nana has been a challenge. And I realize I'm not the most patient person in the world."

"I know your work is stressful," I say, offering her the old way out.

She shakes her head. "That's not an excuse."

I don't know what to say now.

"I guess I just want to say I'm sorry, Reagan. I don't think I've been the best mother—" Her voice breaks slightly. "And that's ironic considering what a perfectionist I am. Anyway, I'd like to try to do better."

Now I do something that I rarely do anymore. I go over and hug her. It's the second time we've hugged tonight and I think it takes us both by surprise. "Me too," I say. "I'd like to try to do better at being a daughter—and a person too. Lately I haven't really liked who I'm becoming."

"But you did the right thing tonight," she points out.

I shrug. "I guess."

I go to bed, but I cannot sleep. Too much is running through my head. I think about Sally, wondering how she's doing. And even though we've had our conflicts, I really do care about her. I really do hope she's okay. Still, it's hard to erase the image of her pale face, her lifeless body. What if she's dead? I can't even imagine that. The only person I know who has died was my grandpa, and I barely remember him. I think about Lisa Carlyle now. She actually is dead. I never knew her, but for some reason it feels like I did. I wonder what she'd be like if she were alive. I wonder if she and I would be friends—if she hadn't died.

I can't stop thinking about death. What really happens when we die? If Sally dies tonight, where will she go? What will she do? What comes next? Or what about Nana? I know she probably won't be around much longer, but what will happen to her? Is death really the end of everything? Do we really just cease to exist? I cannot imagine not existing anymore. How is that even possible? How can I be here now, living, breathing, thinking, hurting . . . and then just be gone? How can that be?

A deep, lonely ache spreads throughout me now. A longing for something—something I can't even describe, something I don't even understand. But it won't go away. I've never really believed in God or much of anything even slightly religious, but suddenly I wish I did. I wish I had what Andrea seems to have. I wish I had something—something much bigger than I am, something much stronger, something I could hold on to. Or something that would simply hold on to me.

I get out of bed and look out the window. I see the dark sky and the stars and I feel so very, very small. I feel like my life is extremely fragile and temporary. I've never really considered my own mortality, but tonight I feel as if I'm looking straight at it. I think about Sally again, imagining how she might be teetering between life and death right now. Or maybe she's already dead. It's all very haunting, very frightening. I don't think I'll ever be able to go to sleep.

I wish I believed in God. And I wish I knew how to pray. As humbling as this is, I wish Andrea were here right now. I wish she would really be my friend and that she would explain to me what it is she has and how she got it. I wonder if I'll feel the same way in the morning. Will the bright light of sunshine burn away all my questions, doubts, and fears? I can only hope.

In the meantime, what if this night never ends?

nineteen

DESPITE GETTING VERY LITTLE SLEEP LAST NIGHT, I WAKE UP FAIRLY EARLY. I am so glad to see the daylight again, so relieved to have that long, dark night behind me. I get out of bed and immediately put together a plan.

First I call the hospital to ask about Sally and Meredith. The woman tells me that Meredith was released to go home last night. But she can't tell me anything about Sally unless I'm immediate family. I consider lying to her, saying that I'm Sally's sister, Betsy. But she probably wouldn't believe me anyway. Besides, I really don't want to be like that anymore. I want to put those things behind me. I want to change.

I wait until after eight to call Andrea. I know this is early for a Sunday, but I also know that her family gets up early since it's their church day. To my relief, Andrea answers the phone.

"I've been praying for you and your friends," she says after I tell her it's me. Then I share the whole story of what happened last night.

"Wow. It's good that you went back there, Reagan."

"Yeah. Except that my friends, rather ex-friends, all hate me now. Well, I can't speak for Sally, since she was unconscious. I still don't know how she's doing. The hospital wouldn't tell me."

"She's probably okay," says Andrea. "They probably pumped her stomach last night and she's probably having breakfast by now."

"I hope you're right."

"And I'm sure she'll be thankful that you did what you did, since it probably saved her life."

"She might be thankful for a few minutes. But when she realizes that I got us all into a bunch of trouble, she'll probably be mad."

"Oh, Sally has her faults, but I think she's got a little integrity too."

Then I tell her about how Kendra was totally furious at me. I even tell her about how I mentioned Lisa to her and she got even madder. "She probably thought I was blaming her for it."

"There was a time when I blamed Kendra for Lisa's death," Andrea admits. "But I finally had to forgive her."

"You forgave her?"

"God helped me forgive her. But I'm glad he did. Not forgiving someone is a real pain—not as much to them as it is to you. I think that's one of the reasons some people are so mean. They need to forgive someone."

I consider this but don't say anything. I wonder if she's talking about me.

"Now, feel free to say no to this, but I wondered if you'd want to go to church with me this morning."

"Okay," I say, surprising myself probably even more than her.

"Great," she says. "Maybe afterward we can swing by the hospital and find out how Sally is doing."

So it is that I find myself sitting in church with Andrea Lynch this morning. And, really, how weird is that? I mean, just last night I was at a drinking party with the "cool" cheerleaders and today I'm in church with Geek Girl. Okay, I'm not calling her that anymore.

That is just plain mean. Still, it seems pretty ironic that I'm here right now. I wonder what Kendra would say.

Another weird thing is that I actually seem to get some of the things the preacher is saying this morning. Besides that, I suspect something very strange is happening *inside* of me. I get this sense that a very real spiritual presence is sort of nudging me, and I think maybe it's God or Jesus or both of them combined. I still haven't sorted out the exact difference between them. According to what the preacher's saying, they really are one and the same. Still, I'm not sure about this. But I am interested.

As we leave, I tell Andrea that I kind of like her church and she seems pleased. And, thankfully, she doesn't pressure me about anything. That's such a huge relief. If there's anything I really don't need right now, it's pressure. I feel like I've had enough pressure these past few weeks to last me a lifetime. Also, I have a feeling that it's not over yet. Maybe it will never be.

After we get in her car, Andrea drives us to the hospital and I ask at the reception desk where Sally's room is. But once we get there, we see that her family is with her, and although we barely get a glimpse into the room, it looks as if she's still unconscious. She has some tubes and things sticking out of her body, and it looks pretty serious, pretty scary too. I'm just backing away from the door when her mother notices me. She immediately comes out, quietly closing the door behind her, and I brace myself, certain I'm about to be blasted for having been involved in the drinking party last night.

"Reagan?" she asks.

I nod without speaking.

"I thought that was you," she says. "I've seen you from a distance at the football games, but I don't think we've actually met. I'm Sally's mother." Then she sticks out her hand and shakes mine. "I want to thank you for calling the paramedics last night."

I just nod, trying to think of something to say. "How is she?" I finally manage to ask.

"She's still in a coma, but they're doing everything they can for her."

A *coma*? Somehow that possibility never occurred to me. But I'm so thankful she's not dead. "I hope she'll be okay." I know that sounds lame, but I really do mean it.

"I'm sure she's going to be fine," she says. "But the doctor told us that Sally would've died if she hadn't gotten medical attention when she did."

I turn to Andrea now, taking a moment to introduce her to Sally's mom, but it turns out they already know each other, back from middle school days. "The truth is," I admit, "I actually left the party early last night, mostly because I didn't want to drink. It was Andrea who helped me realize I needed to go back and make sure everyone was okay."

Sally's mom thanks Andrea too.

"I'll be praying for Sally," Andrea assures her.

"I appreciate that." She pulls out a tissue and uses it to blot a tear.

I wish I could say the same, but I don't even know how to pray.

We tell her good-bye and leave. Neither of us says anything as we go down the elevator, and we are both silent as we walk to her car.

"Do you think Sally's going to be okay?" I finally ask as she drives away from the hospital.

"I don't know," admits Andrea. "It didn't look too good. I plan to call our church and put her on the prayer chain."

"What's a prayer chain?"

"It's a bunch of people who really believe in prayer. One person calls another, and that person calls the next, and before long, there are about fifty people all praying at the same time. We've seen some real miracles as a result."

"Pull over," I say, and Andrea immediately turns on her signal, then pulls over. "Please," I say as I hand her my phone, "call them right now."

So Andrea calls and starts the prayer chain. Then she hands the phone back to me. "We can pray too," she says. And right there, parked on the side of the street, Andrea bows her head and begins to pray. And it sounds like she is talking to a real person.

"Dear heavenly Father," she says, "we're really worried about our friend Sally. Okay, to be honest, she's not actually my friend anymore since she doesn't like me. But I care about her and we used to be friends. Anyway, God, please, please heal Sally. Reach down and put your hand right on her, right now, and heal whatever isn't working inside of her. Whether it's her brain or her lungs or her heart or whatever, I know you know what it is that needs to be touched. I know you can heal what needs to be healed. But, most of all, dear God, please touch her heart and her spirit. Show her how much she needs you, and show her how you love her so much that you sent Jesus so that she could believe in you and never die. Please, God, do a real live miracle for Sally. Amen." Then Andrea opens her eyes, puts her car into gear, and gets back into traffic.

As she drives across town, one line from her prayer keeps reverberating through my head. Finally I have to ask her about it. "Tell me about what you prayed just now — the part about how God loves Sally so much that he sent Jesus so that she could believe in him and never die. What does that mean exactly? How is that possible?"

"It's actually really simple," she says. "There's a verse in the

Bible—in fact, it's the first verse I ever memorized, shortly after I gave my heart to God. Do you want to hear it?"

"Sure."

"I originally learned it from my dad's Bible, but that uses kind of old-fashioned language, so I put it into my own words. It's John 3:16, and this is how it goes: *God loves everyone on earth so much that he sent his only son, Jesus Christ, so that anyone who believes in him will be saved—and they will live forever and never die.*"

"And that's what you really believe?"

"I do."

I consider this, weighing it against the fears I had last night when I was obsessing over life and death and feeling totally confused. And for some reason those words just really resonate inside of me. It's like I really get it.

"So how would I do that?" I finally ask her. "I mean, if I wanted to believe in Jesus too. What would I need to do exactly?"

Andrea sort of laughs, but not in a mean way. "It's easy, Reagan. But let me pull over up here first."

So Andrea pulls onto a side street. "Do you want to pray with me, Reagan? Do you want to ask Jesus into your heart?"

I nod and she explains that she'll pray the words and if I agree with them, I will repeat them afterward. "Basically, you just do it," she says as she bows her head and starts to pray. I echo her words, actually asking Jesus into my heart.

I'm surprised at how simple it really is. And after we're done, I feel this amazing sense of peace. "Wow," I say as I open my eyes.

"Wow?" She looks curiously at me.

"Yeah, I think that took."

She laughs.

"Seriously. I feel like Jesus really is inside of me now."

"Cool!"

I lean back into the seat and let out a big sigh of relief. For the first time in ages—maybe the first time ever—I feel like I can relax. Like the weight of the world isn't sitting on my shoulders. I tell Andrea this and she nods eagerly. "That's because God wants to carry those things for you, Reagan. God wants you to talk to him and to tell him what's worrying you or bugging you. And he wants to help you get through it."

"Wow."

"Yeah." She starts driving again. "You've just started what will be the most exciting journey of your life."

She shares some more things with me and finally asks if I'd like to go visit Nana today. "I was planning on going," she says. "We could go together, if you want."

"Yes!" I say eagerly. "I would love to see Nana. Let's go right now."

So the two of us go into the nursing home together, and although it's just as gloomy and smelly and dreary as the last time I was here, I no longer feel as depressed. I give Nana a big hug, but she doesn't know me at first. She thinks I'm the nurse and asks me if she needs to take a pill. This makes me sad, and I realize it's partly my fault for not having come for a while. It takes a couple of minutes before she remembers who I am, but then her face lights up in a smile.

"It's my Reagan," she says. "Where have you been?"

"Lots of places," I say. Then I tell her all about how I just invited God into my heart and how happy I am about it.

"Yes," says Nana. "Me too."

"You mean you're happy for me?" I ask, somewhat confused. As far as I know, Nana, like me and my mom, has never been particularly religious.

She nods, then taps her chest. "God is in me too."

I glance curiously at Andrea and she just smiles. "That's right, Ruth," she says to Nana. "You did invite God into your heart, didn't you?"

"Yes," Nana says proudly. "I did."

"And have you been talking to God?" asks Andrea. "Have you been telling him how you feel about things?"

She nods. "He brought me breakfast."

Andrea and I both laugh at this. Who knows? Maybe God did bring her breakfast. We stay for about an hour, but I can tell that Nana's getting tired, and I tell her that we should go. Still, it's so good to see her and I'm so glad that we came. I bend down and kiss her soft, wrinkly cheek, promising to come back tomorrow. Then she curls her fingers in that little wave of hers and we go.

twenty

I CAN'T HELP BUT THINK IT WAS NOT A COINCIDENCE THAT SALLY CAME OUT OF her coma about two hours after Andrea's prayer chain started praying for her yesterday. Her mother called to tell me that last night. She sounded extremely relieved and tired. She also said that Sally would remain in the hospital for a few days while they ran some tests. I told her I would continue to pray for Sally.

Today, thanks to the local newspaper, the story of the drunken cheerleaders is all over school. By afternoon, all of the varsity squad cheerleaders except Falon, who is furious, are officially suspended. This means we will not be going to compete at state. Like I care.

"We discussed this a great deal," Coach Anderson tells all of the cheerleaders during seventh-period cheerleading class. "Some people thought we should overlook this infraction. They thought you girls had already learned your lesson. But I feel that we need to adhere to the terms of the contract, and a suspension will be enforced. However, for those girls who are willing to attend an alcohol-diversion class, the suspension will be reduced from four weeks to only two."

The alcohol-diversion class is designed to persuade the attendees that drinking alcohol when underage is both dangerous and wrong. I think we all get that, but we sign up anyway. All except for Sally, that is. It sounds like she won't be at school for the rest of the week.

On Tuesday, Andrea and I go to visit her in the hospital, and we are both shocked at what we see. No longer her talkative, energetic self, this pale, quiet girl in the bed seems like a shadow of the former Sally.

"They've discovered that my heart has some damage," she tells us.

"From the alcohol?" I ask.

"They're not sure. It's possible. Or maybe it was congenital."

"I'm sorry," I say quietly.

She peers curiously at Andrea now, and I can tell she wants to ask what's up with this. So I simply tell Sally that Andrea and I are friends and that I've become a Christian. And she doesn't even seem that surprised.

"My mom told me that you guys were praying for me," she says.

"A lot of people were praying," says Andrea.

"Yeah, thanks."

"When will you be back at school?" I ask.

Sally just shrugs. "Maybe next week. I don't really know. But I do know that I won't be cheerleading ever again."

"Because of the heart thing?"

"Yeah. But I don't really care. It's no big deal."

"I'm really sorry, Sally."

She looks at me now, long and hard, and I wonder if she's still mad at me for taking her place with Kendra. "You know," I tell her, hoping this will cheer her some, "Kendra and I aren't that good of friends anymore." Of course, that's an understatement. Kendra isn't even speaking to me.

"I don't really care about that, Reagan." She sort of laughs, but it has an empty sound. "Kendra won't want to be friends with me either now that I can't be a cheerleader."

"I was actually thinking about quitting myself," I admit.

"Oh, don't do that." Sally frowns. "That's like giving up."

I consider that. I can sort of understand her thinking, but finishing out the year on varsity squad seems like a huge mountain to climb. Still, I know that I should be praying about it. God can show me what's best.

"I wanted to thank you, Reagan," Sally says just before we leave. "I know that you called the paramedics . . . and that I would be dead now if they hadn't come."

"I'm just glad you're okay," I tell her, sharing a little bit about the role Andrea played that night.

"Well, thanks to both of you then." She sighs and leans her head back, closing her eyes.

"And when you're feeling better," I say, "I want to tell you about what happened to me and how I became a Christian. I mean, if you want to hear it."

With her eyes still closed, she almost smiles now. "Yeah, I would like to hear that."

A week later Sally comes to school, and although she seems a little better, she's still not her old self. And by seventh period, she actually looks exhausted.

"Are you feeling okay?" I ask as we walk into the gym together. She's not dressed down like the rest of us, but she says she has an announcement to make.

"Yeah," she says. "It's been a long day."

Sally's announcement is that she's quitting cheerleading. "But that's not all," she says. "I've had some time to think about a few things, and I realize I haven't been a very nice person to many of you. I just want to say that I'm sorry. I also want to say that I wasn't very nice to Jocelyn Matthews when she was on varsity. And I really hope she can take my place now that I have to quit. I know it's not my decision to make, but I hope you'll consider it." She looks at all of us now. "And I think there are a few other girls who need to think about some of the things they've done too." Then she sits down beside me.

"May I say something?" I ask Coach Anderson.

"Certainly."

So I step forward. "I have a confession to make," I say, avoiding Kendra's eyes. "I had something to do with the thing that happened to Jocelyn's uniform at homecoming. I feel really bad about it and I plan to confess it to Jocelyn. But I will totally understand if you want me to step down from cheerleading now. I think that would be fair."

The gym is really quiet now and Coach Anderson clears her throat. "Does anyone else have anything to say?"

A couple of the other varsity squad cheerleaders make some admissions and apologies, including Meredith, who also confesses to being involved in the prank that was pulled on Jocelyn. "I'm sorry," she says. "And I'll apologize to Jocelyn too."

Kendra remains quiet throughout this whole thing. And, judging by her expression, you'd think she's the only one here who is innocent. At first this makes me really angry and I want to blow her cover. Instead, I say a silent prayer and ask God to help me figure out how to handle it. I have a feeling that God wants me to forgive her. If that's the case, he's going to have to help me. But, according to Andrea, that's how he works.

I stop by Jocelyn's house on my way home. Standing at her front door, I confess my part in the uniform mess and tell her that I'm really, really sorry. "I wouldn't blame you for totally hating me."

She doesn't say anything, but I can tell she's mad. And hurt.

"I offered to quit cheerleading," I add. "And if Coach Anderson agrees, you can have my uniform, since we know it'll fit you."

"Sally called me too," she says. "She sort of said the same thing. If everyone keeps confessing and quitting, there won't be a varsity squad left by the end of the week."

"Kendra is the only one keeping her mouth shut."

"Figures."

"Anyway, I really am sorry."

She nods. "Yeah. You said that."

So I take the hint and leave. I think it's understandable that it might take Jocelyn some time to get over this. I just hope she gets reinstated as a cheerleader. I think it's only fair. Not that fair usually happens. Especially in high school. But one can hope.

As it turns out, Coach Anderson takes me aside the following day and tells me that she doesn't plan to remove me from the squad. Of course, this comes with a stern warning. "I'm aware that not all the cheerleaders have been forthcoming about these things." She shakes her head. "Sometimes I just hate this job."

Then Falon announces that we'll vote to see if Jocelyn can be reinstated. Everyone but Kendra votes for Jocelyn to come back. Kendra abstains. "It's a matter of principle," she says. "I just think it was wrong for Jocelyn to swear like that in front of everyone—and at a game. It made us all look bad."

"But it's okay to swear and break the rules and walk all over people as long as you do it secretly?" I ask. A couple of girls snicker and Kendra just rolls her eyes and says, "Whatever."

After our two-week suspension, Jocelyn is back on varsity. She's wearing Sally's uniform, and to everyone's surprise, she and Sally are actually friends. Jocelyn is civilized to me, but that's about it. Kendra treats me like I have cooties. She's also managed to get her old friends back into her court, except for Sally. Meredith is pleased to step into the role of best friend. I am not the least bit envious.

The meanness has subsided some, but I have a feeling it'll be back before long—it's just human nature, or human nature that's allowed to run its course without any God-influence. Because I know God doesn't want us to be mean. I think the meanness is at its worst when people feel insecure or threatened. Not that it excuses their behavior. But it does help me to understand. Still, it's hard to understand why someone like Kendra would feel insecure or threatened when it seems like she has everything. But I guess only God can see into a person's heart.

Andrea and I have been talking to Sally about what it means to be a Christian. And she's been listening and has even agreed to come to youth group with us. Jocelyn has been listening too, but she's got lots of questions and isn't too sure about the whole thing. But I figure there's time. Plus, God can do anything. I know this for a fact because I know what God has done in my life. And I'm really looking forward to what he is going to do in the future. Because every single day I can feel myself changing. Sometimes just a little. Sometimes a lot. And one of the best changes is that I now reach out to the very same kids I used to categorize, ignore, or even snub. And I can see it in their eyes—once they recover from the shock, that is. I can tell that they know I'm changing too.

reader's guide

1. Reagan's internal alarms went off the first time she met Kendra. Why do you think that was?

2. Do you ever have intuitions about potential friends? Are they usually right or wrong? Explain.

3. Why was it important to Reagan that she be counted among Kendra's friends? What did she believe was at stake?

4. How did you feel about Reagan's mother? How do you think the dynamics of Reagan's home life influenced her choices at school?

5. Reagan highly esteemed popularity in her potential friends. What traits do you most treasure in a friend?

6. What was your first impression of Jocelyn? What were her strengths and weaknesses as a friend?

7. What kind of a friend was Reagan? To Jocelyn? To Kendra? To Andrea? What kind of a friend are you? Is there anything you'd like to change?

8. Reagan often said she felt like a hypocrite and became exhausted trying to live up to her friends' expectations. What do these feelings say about the nature of her friendships?

9. How do you define real friendship? What is valid about Reagan's categorization of friends into A, B, and C classes? What is misguided about it?

10. What prompts girls to be mean? Do you think meanness is a sign of strength or weakness?

11. Have you ever been the target of a mean girl? Explain how you felt.

12. Most people are victims of meanness at some point. How do you think God wants you to react when meanness is directed toward you?

about the author

MELODY CARLSON has written over a hundred books for all age groups, but she particularly enjoys writing for teens. Perhaps this is because her own teen years remain so vivid in her memory. After claiming to be an atheist at the ripe old age of twelve, she later surrendered her heart to Jesus and has been following him ever since. Her hope and prayer for all her readers is that each one would be touched by God in a special way through her stories. For more information, please visit Melody's website at www.melodycarlson.com.

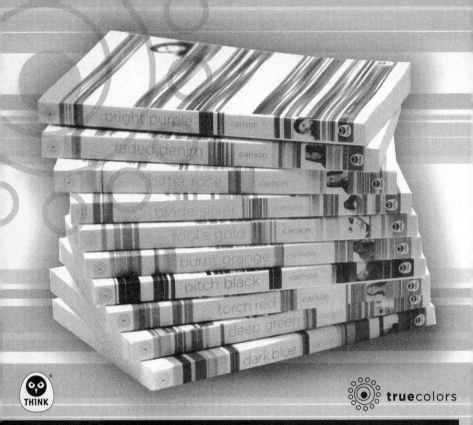

Dark Blue: Color Me Lonely
Brutally ditched by her best friend, Kara feels totally abandoned until she discovers that these dark blue days contain a life-changing secret.
1-57683-529-4

Deep Green: Color Me Jealous
Stuck in a twisted love triangle, Jordan feels absolutely green with envy until her former best friend, Kara, introduces her to Someone even more important than Timothy.
1-57683-530-8

Torch Red: Color Me Torn
Zoë feels like the only virgin on the planet. But now that she's dating Justin Clark, it seems that's about to change. Luckily, Zoë's friend Nate is there to try to save her from the biggest mistake of her life.
1-57683-531-6

Pitch Black: Color Me Lost

Morgan Bergstrom thinks her life is as bad as it can get, but it's about to get a whole lot worse. Her close friend Jason Harding has just killed himself, and no one knows why. As she struggles with her grief, Morgan must make her life's ultimate decision — before it's too late.

1-57683-532-4

Burnt Orange: Color Me Wasted

Amber Conrad has a problem: Her youth group friends Simi and Lisa won't get off her case about the drinking parties she's been going to. Everyone does it. What's the big deal? Will she be honest with herself and her friends before things really get out of control?

1-57683-533-2

Fool's Gold: Color Me Consumed

On furlough from Papua New Guinea, Hannah Johnson spends some time with her Prada-wearing cousin, Vanessa. Hannah feels like an alien around her host — everything Vanessa has is so nice. Hannah knows that stuff's not supposed to matter, but why does she feel a twinge of jealousy deep down inside?

1-57683-534-0

Blade Silver: Color Me Scarred

As Ruth Wallace attempts to stop cutting, her family life deteriorates further to the point that she isn't sure she'll ever be able to stop. Ruth needs help, but will she get it before this habit threatens her life?

1-57683-535-9

Bitter Rose: Color Me Crushed

Maggie's parents suddenly split up after twenty-five years of marriage. The whole situation has Maggie feeling hurt, distraught, and, most of all, violently bitter. She's near desperate for someone who can restore her confidence in love.

1-57683-536-7

Faded Denim: Color Me Trapped

Emily hates her overweight body, her insecure personality, and sometimes even her "perfect" friends. She takes drastic measures to change her body, but the real issues are weighing down her heavy heart.

1-57683-537-5

Bright Purple: Color Me Confused

Ramie Grant cannot believe it when her best friend, Jessica, tells her she's a homosexual. It's just a matter of time before others on the basketball team find out. Quickly, little jokes become vicious attacks. In the end, Ramie must decide if she will stand by Jessica's side or turn her back on a friend in need.

1-57683-950-8

Moon White: Color Me Enchanted

All spirituality is good, right? So says Heather, a teenage girl-next-door, who has recently begun studying the traditions of Wicca. Yet she soon learns that her "harmless" spiritual journey is anything but. In her darkest moment, she discovers hope in a long-lost letter that reconnects her to the truth she's been searching for all along.

1-57683-951-6